FIC   Hebden, Mark,
            1916-

           Pel and the sepulchre
           job.

$17.95

DATE			

PEL AND THE SEPULCHRE JOB

PEL AND THE SEPULCHRE JOB

Mark Hebden

St. Martin's Press
New York

Library of Congress Cataloging-in-Publication Data

Hebden, Mark.
Pel and the sepulchre job / Mark Hebden.
p.   cm.
"A Thomas Dunne book."
ISBN 0-312-09893-6
1. Pel, Evariste Clovis Desire (Fictitious character)—Fiction.
2. Police—France—Burgundy—Fiction.   3. Burgundy
(France)—Fiction.   I. Title.
PR6058.A6886P469   1993
823'.914—dc20   93-29093   CIP

First published in Great Britain by
Constable & Company, Ltd.

First U.S. Edition: December 1993
10 9 8 7 6 5 4 3 2 1

Publisher's Note

Mark Hebden died in March 1991, leaving the
script of *Pel and the Sepulchre Job* unfinished. The
task of completing the book has been undertaken
by Anthony Masters.

Though lovers of Burgundy might decide
they have recognized the city in these pages,
in fact it is intended to be fictitious

PEL AND THE
SEPULCHRE JOB

1

The Arsenal district of the city wasn't an area that the sun smiled much upon. It was a shabby region of old houses and small, not very successful businesses. Through it ran the Canal de Bourgogne, and smack in the centre was the barge port where the barges moored up to load and unload. There were a few warehouses there, a coal hopper, an engineering workshop and a carpenter-boatbuilder's yard where repairs could be made. There were also a few tatty-looking bars where the men who crewed the barges spent their evenings when they were alongside.

Farther along, there was a tarted-up area which was used by the tourist barges and the boats making their way across France by water. But that was different and the vessels that used it were always eyed by the professionals with indifference and contempt. The tourist barges were brightly painted affairs, very different from the drab colours of the working boats. With the season finished, there were no tourist vessels at the moment and the barge crews worked in the first of the daylight to warm up their engines or prepare for a tow.

The dawn had grown into a grey ugly morning with rain and not a lot of light in the sky, and the wind was keen enough for the barge crews to wear more than one jersey. In the air among the whiffs of diesel fumes there was a smell of cooking, and smoke rose from the little tin chimneys above the cabins of the vessels. As the daylight brightened the first barge, *Claudine,* cast off its lines and made ready to move. It was carrying coal and on its wet deck two bicycles were lashed together for the use of its crew ashore. Near them a dog blinked sleepily.

As the engine started, Jean-Louis Casson, the man at the helm, slipped the gear into 'Ahead' and the propeller turned. As he felt the barge stir, there was a shout and he swung round to see the skipper of *Alouette,* the barge next astern, a man called André Parmentier whom he knew as well as he knew most of the barge community, waving frantically at him.

Slipping the engine into neutral, he walked to the stern to see what had happened, wondering if some fool had managed to get a rope round his propeller. Parmentier brushed the rain from his face and pointed at an ugly grey shape that had risen to the surface in the swirling slate-grey water *Claudine's* screw had stirred up. The two men watched it as it moved along the side of *Alouette* and began to bob against the rudder. At first the two men thought it was a bundle of old washing. Then they saw a hand, putty-coloured and unnatural-looking, come into sight as the bundle swayed and turned slowly over. Parmentier laid down the boathook he had been about to use to push the object away from the stern of his vessel and walked slowly to the cabin where his wife was preparing breakfast.

'I'm going to telephone,' he said.

His wife looked up. 'Telephone who?' she asked cheerfully. 'A new girl-friend? An old lover? A bookie to lay a bet?'

'None of them.'

'Then who?'

'The flics.'

His wife looked startled.

'And while I'm gone, just stay in here. Don't go poking around the stern.'

8

'Why not?'

'Never mind why not. Just stay where you are.'

Soon afterwards a police car stopped on the bridge which crossed the canal and the crew began to climb down the muddy bank to the tow-path. *Claudine* had re-moored and Casson and Parmentier were waiting with other men by a sodden grey bundle that lay by the water's edge. Behind them more men in jerseys and women in mufflers and aprons watched from the barges moored to the bollards. The canal was the colour of lead.

'We fished him out,' Parmentier said. He gestured at a grappling hook with a sodden rope at his feet. Behind him a man held a second hook. 'It took four of us.'

'Know who he is?' one of the policemen asked.

'I shouldn't think his own mother would recognize him just now,' Casson said.

The cop was inclined to agree. 'Not one of your lot?' he queried.

'No. We've asked around. Everybody's all present and correct.'

The policeman looked at his companion. 'We'd better get the blood wagon,' he said. 'It seems like a straight-forward suicide.'

'Except', Parmentier said, 'that there's this.'

'This what?'

Parmentier pointed and the policeman frowned and lifted his personal radio.

'Can we go?' Casson asked.

The policeman gestured. 'Not likely,' he said. 'Not just yet.'

Chief Inspector Evariste Clovis Désiré Pel, of the Brigade Criminelle of the Police Judiciaire, didn't like winter. He couldn't understand the need for cold weather. Other countries managed without it; why couldn't France?

9

Knowing how the weather could come down from the east and the uplands of the Plateau de Langres above the city, he was always apprehensive as October turned into November.

It had been a quiet July, August and September. As if all the villains had been on holiday, sunning themselves in the South of France, the Seychelles, Mauritius, the West Indies, Florida, even places like West Africa which once upon a time nobody in his right mind would ever have thought of visiting for pleasure.

According to Pel, only villains could afford to go to such places. Honest men had to make do with staying at home and digging the garden. Pel didn't even do that. When his wife was moved enough by its appearance to suggest a campaign against it, he always found he had a bad leg, a stiff back or files to read.

He had been surprised how quiet his beloved Burgundy had been during the summer months. But at least it meant that an honest cop could enjoy the autumn without getting into a lather chasing crooks; could drink a cool beer at the Bar Transvaal behind the Hôtel de Police, or enjoy a game of boules in the dust under the trees without being interrupted by reports of mayhem, battle, murder and sudden death in one of the city's back streets.

His day had started badly. As he had arrived at the Hôtel de Police to do his daily stint at his desk news had arrived that Judge Polverari, one of the examining magistrates, had died. Examining magistrates, knowing the intricacies of the law, worked closely with the police, questioning suspects, keeping a dossier and generally directing their cases.

Judge Polverari had been one of the good ones and he was an old friend of Pel's. Short and fat and liking the good things of life, he had taken Pel under his wing when he had first arrived, seeing the potential in him when nobody else had. When he had been a penniless inspector, he had treated him occasionally to meals in good restaurants and filled him with the best brandy. He had been away ill for some time but Pel still felt bereft at the news of his death. His only consolation was the knowledge that his place on the examining magistrates' list would undoubtedly be taken by Judge Casteou, his niece, a petite attractive woman who had been standing in for him during his illness.

Everything changed, Pel thought mournfully. Claudie Darel, the only woman in his team, had been married the week before to a barrister from the Palais de Justice and had left. Pel had been fond of Claudie and was already missing her. She had kissed him tearfully at the end of the party the department had thrown for her and told him she'd been happy working for him. It pleased him but it had also startled him because he had always felt nobody could possibly be happy working for Evariste Clovis Désiré Pel. He personally wouldn't have given him house room. Judge Polverari's death, coming on top of Claudie's departure, was the final blow and he was in a doleful mood, a sharp-featured small man with strands of dark hair laid across a balding skull like skid marks on a wet road.

This wasn't particularly unusual, mind you. Doleful moods were as common with Pel as mist in winter. He wasn't exactly a man bursting with. *joie de vivre.* Especially with the rain beating as it was against his window. Still, nothing was ever easy for Pel. He liked it that way. It made him feel he was earning his pay.

He contemplated with sorrow the glowing end of the half-smoked cigarette he held. It was the fifth that morning. He had decided the evening before – for the hundredth time – to give up smoking. He had announced his firm irrevocable decision to his wife. She had regarded it as she regarded most of Pel's doings outside his job as a

11

detective – with wry amusement, quite aware that he was well on the way to becoming an eccentric. Knowing she was able to cope with the fact, however, she never let her amusement show beyond a slight smile. She had passed off the announcement with a wave of her hand and said, 'How wonderful,' knowing perfectly well that, like all the other occasions when he had stopped, it would probably last only until lunch-time the next day.

As he crushed out what was left of the cigarette, there was a tap on the door. It was Daniel Darcy, his inspector and deputy. He was handsome and looked smart, with everything in top gear – clean, bright and lightly oiled. His teeth didn't just shine. They glowed. He always made Pel feel like something the cat had dragged in. He brought with him the daily résumé. It followed the usual pattern: Grievous bodily harm. Drunken driving. Assault. Burglary. All work for Uniformed and Traffic Departments.

'They've also found a floater in the canal,' he ended. 'By the barge port at the Chemin de Chèvre Morte. One of the barge families found him. I expect it's a suicide or a drunk.'

'He picked a nasty night for it,' Pel commented.

'I gather he's been in there some time,' Darcy said. 'He could have come from miles away, moving down the canal as barges passed and locks opened.'

It was later in the day when they learned the name.

'He didn't come from as far away as I thought,' Darcy said. 'His name's Meluc. Robert Meluc. Aged forty-six. Jobbing builder and repairer. Lives at Guincourt and does most of his work here in the city. Doc Minet's got him on the slab. We might know why he was in the water when he's finished with him. It looks like a case of plain suicide by drowning.'

As he finished speaking, Leguyader of the Forensic

Lab appeared with a report and caught the last of his words.

'Drowning's one of the deaths by asphyxia,' he joined in importantly. 'Air's prevented from reaching the lungs and the vital oxygen supply to the brain is cut off.'

The door opened again. This time it was Doc Minet, the police surgeon.

'You can also die of cardiac arrest or from a laryngeal spasm simply from the shock of falling into the water,' Leguyader ended.

Doc Minet smiled and held up his hand like a small boy wanting to leave the classroom. He liked to interrupt Leguyader. They all liked to interrupt Leguyader. Leguyader was clever but he liked people to know it, and made a practice of quoting chunks from the encyclopaedia at them. They suspected he read it all up at night at home to blind the philistines at the Hôtel de Police with science the following day.

'Except', Doc Minet said drily, 'that this one didn't drown. He was dead when he went in. There's no water in the lungs.'

Leguyader shut up abruptly and went out, slamming the door behind him.

Pel looked at the doctor with the trace of a smile. Smiling didn't come easily to Pel but seeing Leguyader discomfited made the effort worth while. The smile died. Doc Minet's report had changed things quite considerably.

'How long was he in the water?'

Minet smiled. 'Over thirty-six hours. After a few hours in the water the skin on the hands works in a fashion known as "washerwoman's hands". Which means it takes on a bleached and wrinkled appearance. But you know this already. It isn't necessarily an indication of death by drowning, only of how long he's been in the water. In this case it's very well developed.'

Pel frowned. 'So if he didn't drown, how did he die?'

Minet's smile faded. 'There are holes in his head. What looks like an entrance and exit wound. That means a bullet. I'll tell you more when I've examined him more closely. I just thought you'd like to know at once.'

It was late in the afternoon as Pel sat with Darcy at a table in the Café Marine, a bar near the canal, and started asking the barge crews if anybody had seen anything. Nobody had.

'Most of us start early,' Parmentier explained. 'So our lights usually go out about ten o'clock. If it happened after that nobody would see a thing.'

Judge Casteou made her statutory visit to the scene, taking a *café fine* with Pel and Darcy against the chill in the little brown-and-drab bar. The proprietor's wife produced a decent cup for her, not one of the thick ones the barge families were usually offered, and gave the glass for the brandy an extra polish.

By evening they had a little more.

'He'd been in there for around six days,' Doc Minet decided. 'With the weather as it is, it's hard to be certain. I'm guessing.'

'Any indication of who did it?' Pel growled.

Doc Minet shrugged. 'None whatsoever. The bullet was a 6.35. But I'm still guessing. We didn't find it. No other marks on the corpse to indicate anything unusual. No marks of ropes. No marks of gags. No marks of strangulation or garrotting. But with a bullet in the head, there doesn't appear to have been much need for anything extra, does there?'

Darcy sent Aimedieu out to Guincourt to see the dead man's widow and they got the frogmen out to search the canal for the weapon. The owner might just have tossed it into the water at the same time as he had tossed Meluc in. But they found nothing. They didn't really expect to, but the usual motions had to be gone through. In fact, the gun was probably lying in long grass in a hedge bottom somewhere or had been broken down with a sledge-hammer into small and unnoticeable pieces and dumped in a dustbin. Guns being expensive, it might even still be in the possession of the owner who could well be thinking of using it again on someone else.

Since the body had been found in the canal at a point near the district of Arsenal, they made enquiries in that area, but nothing emerged. Again, they didn't even know they were searching in the right place. The canal passed close to Guincourt and the body might have drifted along, stirred from one place to another by the movement of water as locks were opened.

Late in the evening, Aimedieu arrived back from Guincourt. He had obtained a photograph of Meluc. He laid it on Pel's desk. It showed a short broad-shouldered man in overalls standing in front of a large van.

'Taken about six months ago, Patron,' he said.

'Find out anything about him?' Pel asked.

'He's got a record. Involved in a bank hold-up in Reims. Did two years. He was the driver.'

'Has his wife anything to say about him being dead?'

'Only that she's glad. She didn't say so in so many words but it obviously doesn't worry her much. He was a bit of a drunk and knocked her about. She'd been thinking of leaving him for some time.'

'Has she any idea who might have done it?'

'None at all, Patron.'

'What about his friends?'

'She doesn't know them. He spent all his spare time here in the city. She was always glad when he was out of the house. She never saw him with friends because she thinks they were all here. In the city. She thinks some of them were crooks.'

15

'Judging by the fact that he's dead, she could be right. Anybody threatened him? Anything like that?'

'Nothing she knows about, Patron. There was just one thing. He had a blue van. The one in the picture. A Renault. Number 1467-RL-69. He used it for his work and it was full of equipment. Bags of cement, tiles, bricks – that sort of thing. Together with his tools. His ladders were on top. It's not at Guincourt. So it must be somewhere around.'

Pel nodded. It all seemed a routine matter and a pall of boredom hung over him. The day felt too long.

2

So that was that. They had a dead man on their hands and they had no idea why. But when people with records were found in water with gunshot wounds in the head it was always a good idea to look into the circumstances because the chances were that they'd been dumped. Different crooks, different methods. Down in Marseilles and Nice they preferred to wrap them in concrete and dump them in the sea. But either way it was always a good idea to try to find out why.

Pel set into motion a number of enquiries that were made around the city bars and copies of the photograph of Robert Meluc were shown. A few bartenders recognized him but none of them knew him well. He seemed to have been a man who had kept very much to himself. They found a few people he'd worked for but it didn't lead them on very much. And when they failed to discover any trace of the van they decided that for some reason not yet known to them it had been deliberately hidden, and that finding out why Meluc was dead and who had killed him was going to be a long-drawn-out job.

Had the van been used to transport something illegal such as drugs? It seemed very likely.

Then Doc Minet produced a plastic bag containing the contents of Meluc's wallet and they found themselves more deeply in the mire.

'One hundred and fifty francs,' Doc Minet said. 'Wet and difficult to separate. Driver's licence. Bank card. And something that might well interest you. A puzzle for you to solve.'

On the table he laid a sheet of paper, dry now but showing signs of having been soaked. 'Being folded in his wallet preserved it,' Doc Minet said.

'What is it?' Darcy asked.

It was a xerox of a simple drawing, but the drawing resembled nothing they recognized – a collapsing tent seemed the most likely. Written beneath the drawing in what was clearly a hurried hand was a date, 3 December.

Pel reached lethargically for his desk diary. 3 December seemed not to suggest anything untoward. It indicated a conference with the Chief and heads of departments about staffing and recruitment but nothing more.

'Why 3 December?' he asked.

Nobody knew.

'Better make a note, Daniel,' Pel suggested. 'It obviously means something to someone.' He peered again at the drawing. 'If it's not a ray,' he said, 'which seems unlikely, what's the crooked line attached to it?'

'If it's a tent, can that be one of the guy ropes? And what's this curved line at the side?'

Inevitably they took it to Leguyader, who pounced on it at once, anxious to recoup some of the kudos he had lost.

'It looks like a ray,' he said.

'A what?'

Leguyader smiled. 'Ray,' he said. 'Term applied to the elasmobranch fishes, which are distinguished by their flattened bodies and enormous expanded pectoral fins. The gill-slits are on the under-surface of the head while the eyes are on the top. They're roughly this shape and have a long tail.'

He took a book from a shelf and showed them the picture of a ray. It was certainly similar in outline to the drawing Doc Minet had found, except that the tail was longer and thicker.

'I'm told they can be dangerous, these tails,' Leguyader said. He frowned at the drawing. 'It does look remarkably like a ray. Except that there are too many corners, too many small excrescences that shouldn't be there. Fishes are remarkably well streamlined. And the eyes are at the wrong end.'

Since Burgundy was about as far from the sea as you could get in France, it confirmed their fixed belief – the fixed belief of everybody in the Hôtel de Police – that Leguyader read the *Encyclopédie Larousse* every night. He could hardly have seen a ray in the River Orche and they all knew his weekend house was not on the coast. Leguyader had what he called a delicate stomach that made him feel seasick even in the bath.

Nevertheless, they had to hand it to him. The outline found in Robert Meluc's wallet did resemble a ray. It even had a tail and the tail was in roughly the right place.

'Why would he want the drawing of a ray?' Darcy asked.

'It seems to have been important,' Pel remarked. 'Otherwise, why did he keep it and why has it been xeroxed? Xeroxing implies that several copies are needed. Why are several copies of *this* needed? Keep it, Daniel. Have it xeroxed again and have it shown around. Somebody might recognize what it is and why he was carrying it.'

Because things were quiet, they continued to study the copies of the xeroxed drawing. Sometimes it resembled a ray, sure enough, but at other times a rather crude star.

'Think it's some kind of symbol?' Darcy asked.

'What have you in mind?'

'Don't these people who go in for satanic rites use a goat's horns?'

'It doesn't much resemble a goat's horns to me. If it reminds me of anything, it's a kite.'

'A crude drawing of a flower? The tail thing is the stalk.'

It occupied them for some time, then at the end of November the quiet period which had preceded the death of Robert Meluc suddenly sprang to life with a bang. It was as though all the crooks, having returned from their holidays to settle down for the winter, felt as though they needed to earn some money to pay for the good times they'd had. Before they knew where they were, the police were up to their eyeballs in work and Robert Meluc became submerged in other things.

To Pel the days became shorter, jam packed with ominous action; it was as though France had suddenly become a hotbed of crime. You'd only to look at the newspapers. They contained every crime in the calendar: murder, arson, extortion, embezzlement, breaking and entering, indecent behaviour, rape, assault and battery, pimping, offences against public morals, non-payment of taxes, acid throwing, bomb planting, drug pushing, permitting the emission of lethal fumes from a factory, the sale of drinks to minors, adulteration of eatables, driving under the influence, not declaring the contents of food, counterfeiting, smuggling, perjury, incitement to desertion, non-assistance of persons in danger, robbery with violence, threats, sedition, attack with an offensive weapon, drunk in charge of a perambulator. They were all there. Even stealing a garden gnome. There were photographs, too, when the *paparazzi* had managed to get near enough, pictures of victims well smeared with blood. It was enough to make you weep when you thought about it. The best thing, of course, was not to think about it. But that wasn't easy when you were a cop.

In Pel's parish it started with a break-in at Sobelec, the premises of Henri Sobène, who sold televisions, videos, computers and all their accessories. Henri Sobène was proud of his shop. Leaving school at sixteen, he had been apprenticed to an electronics engineer and had quickly assimilated the techniques. He had then worked for a few years selling and repairing electronic devices before deciding he had enough knowledge to set up on his own. Sobelec was the result. He had named it Sobelec because he thought Henri Sobène, Videos, Electronic Games and Televisions was too much for a customer to remember, to say nothing of the fact that it took up too much room when writing a cheque. It would also cost a fortune to have it painted across the top of his window. The name, he felt, made his place different from all the other shops in the city selling electronic gadgets. They were called Gadelec, Annexelec, Langelec, Jeunelec, Rubelec and Aselec.

He had found the premises, requested a loan from the bank and acquired stock. He was now doing splendidly and his shop was crammed with televisions, videos and computers that worked electronic games for children. The only snag was that the premises were barely large enough for his expanding business. There was also the problem of the double yellow no-parking lines in the road outside and he was looking for a new shop with better access because the only people who were allowed to stop long enough to study his window were people with disabled stickers on their windscreens. People with disabled stickers, however, were on the whole elderly and not interested in new-fangled devices.

Nevertheless, on the morning of 2 December, one such car was parked outside the shop just before the morning rush started. A traffic warden, fresh on her rounds from headquarters and eager to cop someone, saw it from the rear. Her feet were cold and she was in a bad temper and the thought that passed through her mind was a triumphant 'Got 'em.' She was duly disappointed when she saw the disabled ticket with the cripple-in-a-wheelchair symbol on the windscreen. The traffic warden moved on. Two pairs of eyes watched her vanish round the corner, then the owners of the eyes hurried out of the shop, climbed into the car, removed the disabled ticket and drove off.

That morning Pel had woken warily, expecting the day to attack him. He was dead right. It started to rush at him the minute he arrived in his office and his lethargy of a few days ago was gone.

'There's been a punch-up in a bar at Bezay,' Darcy announced. 'Well, less of a punch-up than a pitched battle. Four injured, plus the type who started it. It's hard to tell who came off worst. The proprietor of the bar has a fractured jaw and three of his customers have various injuries. The type who started it seems to have wiped the floor with them. And they're tough types round Bezay – quarry workers and that sort. All he got was a broken ankle. And he got that trying to jump over a table that collapsed under him. It's a job for Uniformed. Charges are being preferred. Name of Georges Guillet. He's in a private ward in the Hospital of the Sacred Heart, Uniformed has a man watching him.'

Pel pushed his spectacles up on to his forehead. 'Are they expecting him to escape?'

'It seems he has a twin brother and he's expected to try to get him out. You know what twins are.'

'Are these two dangerous?'

'Uniformed don't know. They're exactly alike and they do a comic act in a circus that's running at Bezay, whereby one man seems to be in two places at once. Uniformed's been out to the circus. They say François Guillet, the brother, is a hot-tempered type and is devoted to *our* Guillet. But they say it's normal enough.'

2 December had arrived on time. As he noticed the date, Pel felt like Julius Caesar keeping an eye on the Ides of March. With a certain unease they had been watching the days ever since the middle of November. They still hadn't found the meaning of the strange diagram from Meluc's pocket but the date was clear. It meant something, as the diagram undoubtedly did.

Perhaps the diagram was only a child's scrawl – though it looked too confident for a child. Perhaps it was drawn to show a child how to make a kite. But if so, where were the most important parts – the struts that braced it? It might have been only somebody's birthday, jotted down as a reminder. It might indicate that someone's car was due for a service, or a woman was due to visit her hairdresser. It might be any of a thousand things, but they were all aware it might also indicate the beginning of something they didn't fancy facing. A riot. A bomb for the President outside the Elysée Palace. They had checked with the Prefect and contacted the Elysée Palace to put the guard on alert just in case.

'Circus people tend to be very close. They say he's gone missing.'

Darcy broke into Pel's thoughts, glancing at the file in his hands. 'There's been one other crime – a break-in at Sobelec. That's the big television and video shop in the Rue Aristide Briand. Morell's there. A television, a video, twelve cassettes and two computers have been stolen. Morell picked up a discarded disabled ticket. He thought it was unusual. The disabled cling to those things as if they're diamonds because they mean they can park anywhere.'

'So are geriatrics going into the smash and grab business?'

'It was home-made. You can't park outside Sobelec so it's pretty clear that whoever did it used it so they wouldn't be disturbed. The fact that computer games have gone suggests kids.'

'Driving cars?'

'Kids of fifteen', Darcy said, 'are big enough and strong enough and clever enough these days not only to drive cars but also to understand electronics. It looks to me as if they pinched the television and video to raise money and the games to amuse themselves. Kids are crazy about them and in the amusement arcade in the Rue de Rouen it costs five francs a go. The fact that they can draw a phoney disabled ticket suggests they might be good at art. Morell says the sticker's good enough to deceive all but a close look and it seems a traffic warden passed by around that time without noticing anything odd.'

Darcy closed the file and looked up. 'By the way,' he said, 'Claudie's replacement's arrived.'

Pel drew a deep breath. He wasn't against women police officers. At times they were a definite asset and in any case the law these days demanded them. Women could handle delicate enquiries about things like rape, sexual harassment, marital troubles, children. Claudie had been good at them. This one might be different. She also might look like the back of a bus.

'What's she like?' he asked.

'That's something we'll have to find out, Patron.'

'I meant, what does she look like?'

Darcy gave nothing away. 'You'd better take a look at her, Patron,' he said. He pushed his pack of Gauloises across the desk and Pel snatched one hungrily. He drew in smoke and for a while allowed it to drift round his sinuses and various other tubes. It was like running a flue brush through them.

'Show her in,' he growled.

The young woman who appeared was unusual. She was small with a face like an excited elf, flaming red hair and brilliant green eyes. After Claudie, who was dark, calm and looked like a young Mireille Mathieu and had had everyone in the Hôtel de Police falling in love with her in droves, she was unexpected to say the least. Her mouth was too wide, her nose not the right shape and she had an aggressive look about her. After Claudie she was not at all what they'd hoped for and Pel looked at her as if she might bite.

He shook hands with her, then she sat in the chair Darcy pushed forward.

'Better have your name,' Pel muttered.

'Saxe,' she said. 'Anne-Marie Saxe. They call me Annie.'

'Saxe,' Pel said, trying to be friendly. 'Proud name. There was a Marshal Saxe.'

'No relation,' the girl said sharply. 'He was born in Germany.'

'Where do you come from?'

'Haute-Levette, Belfort.'

'This is Burgundy,' Pel said and Darcy knew exactly what he meant.

To Pel if you stepped outside Burgundy you were in danger of falling into an abyss. Burgundians were known for their pride in their province and Pel was the Burgundian of all Burgundians. According to Pel there was only one wine in France – all those produced outside Burgundy could only be used as medicine. Burgundy also produced famous men and women: Bussy-Rabutin. Vauban. Lamartine. Colette. Pel.

'Why did you apply to come here?' he asked the girl.

'I heard that round here people know something about police work. I do shorthand.'

Pel sniffed. Pel's sniff could say a lot. 'You're not very big,' he pointed out.

She gave him a sharp look. 'If I can do what bigger people do,' she retorted, 'that makes me as big as they are. And, with respect, sir, you're not all that big yourself. But I've heard you know what you're about.'

Pel glanced at Darcy. Darcy hurriedly concealed a smile.

'We get a lot of work here,' Pel said. 'Think you can stand the pace?'

'Belfort', she pointed out, 'was still holding out against the Prussians in 1871 when the rest of France had surrendered. When Alsace was annexed by the Germans, Belfort was allowed to remain French in tribute. We have a statue of a lion to commemorate the defence. It faces east to Germany. In defiance.'

Pel looked nonplussed and Darcy stepped in hurriedly. 'If I were you,' he said, 'I should have a word with Claudie Darel. Her new husband's taken a job in Paris and she'll be going with him. But it's not for a month or so and she's still around. She might be able to tell you what happens here.'

And about Pel, too, he decided. Which was something. Getting used to Pel required a major effort.

Fortunately, Claudie and Pel had always got on well together, so perhaps her report on him would be a good one. He studied the girl seated at Pel's desk. As Pel had said, she wasn't very big but she seemed to have spirit enough for two. Which was as well because there were other hazards around the Hôtel de Police in the shape of lecherous cops. Among them Josephe Misset, Pel's *bête noire*. Once upon a time Misset had been a handsome young cop. Now he was a middle-aged cop with a belly from too much beer drinking and a habit of chasing girls.

He liked his wife as much as he liked hell and spent most of his spare time hanging round bars chasing spare bits of skirt. 'Keeping the old ears open,' he liked to explain to his family to excuse his absence in the evenings.

Pel was still studying the newcomer warily. 'You're here on probation, of course,' he pointed out. 'Two months for a start. If at the end of it you don't come up to our standards you go back to Belfort. Understood?'

The girl stiffened as if she were on parade. 'I understand.'

'If you measure up you stay. All right?'

'All right. Sir.'

As the door closed, Darcy turned to Pel. 'You were a bit tough with her, Patron,' he said.

'She's got too much bounce.'

'Cops need bounce. Self-confidence does no harm.'

'Self-confidence sometimes gets them killed. I prefer them alive. They're more useful that way.'

'You didn't put Claudie through that sort of routine.'

Pel sniffed. 'Claudie was different,' he said.

'I'll introduce you to everybody,' Darcy said as he met the girl in the corridor outside. She appealed to him. Give her a few days, he thought, and if she were any good – and Darcy had a feeling she would be – Pel would back her to the hilt.

He fished out of his pocket a small booklet printed in black and orange on white. It contained a list of streets, hotels, restaurants, transport and a detailed map of the city.

'I'd advise you to get hold of one of these as soon as you can,' he said. 'It's a Plan-Guide Blay. It covers the city and the suburbs. One of the district around would help, too, but this is the most important. Plan-Guides Blay produce them of every city in France.'

'We've got one of Belfort.'

'Every sensible cop carries one. It's not a matter of official police instruction but it's pure common sense. It not only impresses tourists because it enables you to answer their half-baked queries, it also enables you to find the quickest route to any nest of criminal activity. You can buy them at any newspaper shop. Despite their value to us, the powers that be do *not* believe in providing them free of charge.'

In the sergeants' room, Nosjean and De Troq' were bending over a desk studying a report. They often worked together and were known as the Heavenly Twins. Nosjean looked like the young Napoleon on the bridge at Lodi. De Troq' – Baron Charles Victor de Troquereau Tournay-Turenne, the only cop Darcy knew with a title – was small, neat, with a perfect haircut and smart clothes. His family was supposed to be poor but poverty seemed to be a comparative thing because De Troq' drove a car the size of a zeppelin with a strap over the bonnet, headlamps like a lighthouse and wheels like an airliner. He was currently escorting a girl who worked in the Palais de Justice whose family also had a title. Unlike De Troq's, their title was only a Second Empire creation but, De Troq' felt, it would do for the time being.

Misset was there, too, smooth and oily behind the dark glasses he affected. With him were Brochard and Aimedieu, two more bright boys from Pel's squad, and Lage, the golden oldy, who was close to retirement but was still their expert on intricate cases that didn't require a lot of inspiration but did call for a great deal of sheer hard graft. There was also Debray, who had taken a course on computers and had a gift for looking anonymous, a not invaluable asset in a plain-clothes cop, and Lacocq and Morell, the last arrivals in the squad. There was also Bardolle, their heavy man, as wide as he was high with a voice like a foghorn. He looked like the wicked giant out of a fairy story but when he smiled he was more like the sort of traffic warden who crossed the road with infants hanging on his arms like bunches of grapes. Finally there was Cadet Darras, who was a protégé of Pel's.

They were a mixed bunch, Darcy thought as he introduced them. 'This is Annie Saxe,' he said. 'She's come to take Claudie's place. She's from Belfort.'

'They say that in that part of France,' Misset observed with the smooth smile of a ladykiller, 'they're as thick as their own trees.'

She gave him a cold smile, and they crowded round her, asking questions, sizing her up.

'Belfort's a bit out-of-the-way,' Misset went on from a position behind her. 'Nothing much to do round there, I should think.'

'I found plenty,' Annie Saxe retorted. 'When I was younger I played rugby with my brothers.'

'I should think you got knocked about a bit.'

'Not really. There were five of them and they taught me a few things about looking after myself. Some of them very painful. I use them on men who consider my backside free pasturage for their hands.'

Misset drew his hand back as if she'd been red hot.

'She's arrived,' Pel announced when he reached home that night and stood in the hall shaking the rain off his hat.

Madame Routy, the housekeeper with whom he had kept up a running skirmish for years, took his briefcase and placed it beside the table in the hall. She looked at Pel as if he were a terrorist who had brought home a homemade and not very stable bomb. She had been Pel's housekeeper before his marriage and had been taken on with Pel, lock, stock and barrel. He wiped his feet with elaborate energy to make sure she noticed.

'Who's arrived?' Madame Pel said, appearing from the study.

'The new help. Claudie's replacement.'

'What's she like?'

'A bit like a red-haired rat.'

Madame frowned. 'You shouldn't say things like that, Pel,' she admonished gently. 'I'm sure she isn't.'

'She comes from Belfort.'

'That's a brave city.'

'It's to do with being close to Switzerland. They don't think much round that way. She's probably got Swiss relatives.'

Madame remained unconvinced. 'I'm sure she's not half as bad as you think. Perhaps we ought to have her in for a meal.'

'No,' Pel yelped.

'We had Claudie.'

'Claudie was different.'

'This one might be, too, given a chance. You must remember she's probably nervous. She's a long way from home in a new city with new colleagues. She's even probably very lonely.'

Pel felt humbled enough to throw himself at his wife's feet.

Madame was pouring him a whisky now and he took a sharp look at the bottle. With Pel humility didn't last long. He had taken his wife out to dine the night before and at such times, he felt, Madame Routy took advantage of their absence to help herself. He hadn't quite got to the point of marking the level with a pencil but he liked to keep an eye on it. It wasn't that he was mean, he felt. It just paid to be careful.

The meal that appeared was excellent with a fine Chambertin, the wine beloved of Napoleon. If it were good enough for the First Emperor, Pel felt, it ought to be good enough for Evariste Clovis Désiré Pel.

'Splendid meal,' he remarked.

'Madame Routy,' his wife pointed out.

'*She* did it?'

'Yes.'

'Why did she never cook meals like this when she was my housekeeper before we were married?'

His wife gave one of her cheerful little smiles and said nothing. She had a special gift of calmness, of being able to say nothing when so many wives would have claimed some responsibility for the miracle. It was just another of her qualities, like having the perception to realize how Pel hated his Christian names. It had taken her no more than a few weeks to start calling him simply 'Pel'. You couldn't muck about with that much and it saved endless bad temper and made her seem very wise. Pel considered himself very lucky to have her and could only put it down to the fact that she was slightly short-sighted and must have fallen for him when not wearing her specs. His hope was that he would continue to get away with it.

He slept badly that night. The meal gave him indigestion and he was pleased he could blame Madame Routy for something. But there was something else, too. What his wife had said had begun to trouble him and he was worried that he had reacted badly to Annie Saxe's arrival. After all, he thought, she wasn't very old and was probably only lacking in experience. In addition, she came from the border area which for almost fifty years after the disaster of the war against the Prussians had been part of Germany. Her red hair probably even indicated that somewhere in their past, one of the family had mated with a German. But, however he looked at it, he couldn't bring himself to like her name. It sounded like a rifle shot instead of running off the tongue like

'Claudie Darel'. And she didn't look like Mireille Mathieu.

He shifted restlessly on his pillow and tried to dismiss his criticisms with the thought that he was probably being biased – even racist. He eventually settled himself to sleep with the decision that the following morning he would make up to her by being as nice as possible. He would smile at her in a kindly way – he was unaware that his kindly smiles were enough to frighten a paratrooper – compliment her on what she was wearing, and generally behave like a Dutch uncle.

He woke in a bad temper, relieved to see the rain had stopped because, when it rained, he was always convinced he'd got rheumatism.

The first thing he did was switch on the television for the early morning news. Madame raised her eyebrows, knowing he detested television at breakfast time, but she suspected there was method in his madness.

'3 December,' he said. 'I wondered if anything had happened yet.' He had discussed the date with her, as he discussed all his cases. 'It's today.'

'Do you think it meant anything?'

'I don't know. That's why I'm listening to the news.'

But the news provided no clues to the meaning of the strange diagram or the date written on it. The President was meeting the Prime Minister of Britain. The farmers in the south were complaining again. The Middle East wouldn't go away. Thank God the Russians had discovered what a lot of crooks their leaders had been and finally settled to being part of a world community. But there was nothing that indicated why 3 December was important. Most of what was on the news was part of the ongoing scene. It seemed safe to go to the office.

As usual, his wife cheerfully prepared to leave for her

own office in the Rue de la Liberté where she ran a hairdressing salon whose prices were enough to frighten away all but the wealthiest. Alongside, in case her clients had anything left after paying for their hair, she had opened an expensive boutique and not far away a teenagers' shop, a sportswear shop, a children's wear shop and a shop selling denim. She was now thinking of branching out and selling shoes. Probably eventually, Pel often thought, there would be houses, limousines, transatlantic liners. It made him feel ashamed to be only a policeman but at least it reassured him that his future after retirement would be secure.

As he picked up his briefcase, the telephone went. Pel snatched it up and glared at it as if he expected a mouse to jump out of it. 'Pel,' he snarled.

'Annie Saxe here, sir.'

He had forgotten his resolutions of the night before. 'What do *you* want?' he barked.

'The Chief said you ought to come in at once.'

'Why?'

'He doesn't tell me things like that. Sir.'

'This is the morning when I don't come in till later. Everybody knows that.'

'Then it's a pity – sir – nobody thought to tell *me*.' The comment came back, brisk and defiant.

Pel considered the request. It didn't seem to have anything to do with anything threatening. But it *was* 3 December and this might mean something.

'Let him know I'm on my way,' he said.

Madame saw him off. She studied his car. It was small and growing old. He had had it ever since his marriage and had only bought it then because Madame had finally refused to be seen dead in his old one. The doors of that one had deposited oil on her clothes and didn't fasten properly so that she was in danger of being dumped in the gutter every time they rounded a corner.

33

'I think you need a new car, Pel,' she said mildly.

Pel looked round in alarm. It was only seven years – well, nearly eight – since he had bought the one he was sitting in.

'Think of your position,' his wife said.

It was the iron fist under the velvet glove.

'Cars cost money,' he pointed out.

'We've got plenty,' his wife urged. 'Between us we've got quite a lot. Treat yourself. Spend some of it. It'll make room in the bank for the next lot that comes in.'

It was a hard argument to counter.

As he switched on the engine, he saw Yves Pasquier, the small boy from next door, looking at him through a hole in the hedge. It was through this hole that they conducted most of their conversations. Judging by the bruises, cuts and scratches on his legs, Pel would have said the boy had had a fight with a motor mower. He was accompanied by his dog. It was shaggy enough for Pel to be unable to tell which was the end that bit.

'Off to work?' the boy asked.

'Yes,' Pel admitted. He always respected the interest of any small boy in police work because it sometimes led him to want to be a policeman himself when he grew up.

'Anything big on at the moment?' Yves liked to be kept *au fait* with what was happening at the Hôtel de Police.

'Not much.' Pel knew he was being optimistic. Demands for his presence from the Chief didn't seem to indicate not much.

Yves grinned. 'Perhaps', he said, 'all the gangsters have gone on strike.'

Well, Pel thought as he drew away, there could always be a first time.

When he reached the city, police sirens were going and Pel realized at once that 3 December was living up to the threat suggested by the scrawl on the strange diagram from Meluc's wallet. He had been too optimistic by a long way.

There was no policeman at the Porte Guillaume, but there was a whole group of them at the junction of the Rue Bossuet and the Rue de la Liberté and, he noticed, they were all armed, yet the usual man outside the Hôtel de Police was missing. It looked ominous.

Inside he found uproar. Policemen seemed to be dashing in all directions and every telephone in the building appeared to be ringing. The sergeants' room was empty except for Annie Saxe who was sitting by the telephone, umbrage written all over her face. She had obviously taken offence at the way he had answered her call to his home.

'What's going on?' Pel asked.

'Hostage situation,' she said. 'Banque Crédit Rural de Bourgogne.'

Pel understood at once what the date on the scrawled diagram meant. It had been the day for what was now happening at the Banque Crédit Rural de Bourgogne and the diagram had some connection with it. He also understood why the Chief had been so cagey about the method of calling him in. Bank hold-ups and hostage situations weren't things the police liked to have bruited about.

'When the staff arrived,' Annie Saxe was saying, 'they found the premises occupied. The report at the moment is that there are four of them. They're holding sixteen staff. They collared them one by one as they arrived. The manager was last and they threatened to do for his wife and children. He handed over the keys. While they were busy in the vaults, though, somebody managed to get to a telephone and Uniformed have surrounded the place. Reinforcements are on their way. All leave's stopped. Uniformed checked at the manager's home. The family are safe but a guard's been put on the house. The manager and the staff are being held as hostages. There's been shooting.'

It was a brief but admirable report.

'Who's handling it?'

'Uniformed Branch. It's their affair, I suppose.'

The answer was sulky but Pel had to admit that this one was brighter than he had imagined. It certainly *was* Uniformed Branch's affair. He supposed that the Chief had been called in and would take over. Turgot, who ran Uniformed, would be there, too, biting his nails and wondering how best to tackle it.

'Where's everybody?'

'Inspector Darcy thought he'd better have a look, in case we were called in. He didn't think we would be. Everybody else's out.'

'Why are you on the telephone? Misset should be handling calls.'

'He said he'd better go and have a look, too.'

He would, Pel thought.

'I expect Uniformed are making a mess of things,' he said. 'But it's their pigeon. Still, I'd better put in an appearance. If only for the look of the thing. Get hold of someone to sit on the phone. You'd better come with me. It'll help you get to know the city.'

She gave him a grin that changed her whole face. From being sullen, defiant and challenging it suddenly filled with sunshine. It rocked Pel back on his heels.

'Right, sir,' she said.

'Can you drive?'

'Not half.'

'What does that mean?'

'Like the wind, sir.'

'I hope it doesn't,' Pel said gravely. 'I'm of a distinctly nervous disposition. Get the car. I'll meet you outside.'

3

The Banque Crédit Rural de Bourgogne was situated on the edge of an area of narrow streets near the Church of St Philibert. It occupied part of a block of offices in a small open space that wasn't quite a square but also wasn't quite a street, though it was called the Rue de la Queste. Clubbed acacias, empty of leaves, grew from iron gratings outside, and on the edge of the pavement there was one of the tall round pillars leading to the sewers, plastered over with theatrical posters, gaudy placards advertising ancient rock concerts, football matches and the summer's fairs, cassoulets and sardinages, as well as just plain graffiti, sprayed on, chalked or stuck on.

Cars were parked anyhow, but there weren't many because the entrances to the area had been blocked off with steel barriers and police vans drawn up crosswise across the highway. There wasn't a soul in sight but there were plenty of people around, mostly police, keeping their heads down behind cars, vans and walls. Inspector Turgot, of Uniformed, a tall, handsome man, looked worried. He had only recently taken over the job after the death of his predecessor and it was his first big occasion. Rifles were obvious everywhere, with loudhailers and electronic equipment.

The Chief was there, too, looking as if he could chew the heads off nails. He was talking to Inspector Pomereu, of Traffic, whose men were handling the barriers and the snarl-up of cars they were causing.

'This isn't the sort of thing we expect here,' the Chief growled.

'What *is*?' Pel asked.

'There's been shooting.'

'Much?'

'Three shots. They hit the roof opposite.'

'Not very *good* shots.'

'They appear to be warnings to us to keep our distance. They obviously mean business. They've got hostages.'

Pel nodded. Hostages were the latest element in the everlasting game of cops and robbers. If your heist went wrong and you found yourself in trouble, you collared a hostage or two and used them to bargain for your freedom.

'Ought we to get the CRS boys in?' the Chief asked.

'No,' Pel said immediately. He didn't like the special emergency groups. 'We should handle it ourselves.'

'They like to be called in for major events.'

'This is a *local* event.'

The Chief nodded, lit a cigarette and offered the packet to Pel. Pel accepted, aware that, with Claudie Darel's departure, Judge Polverari's death and this new emergency, his stout assertion that he was giving them up had long since flown out of the window.

'Anywhere we can talk?' the Chief asked.

'Café St Michel at the end of the street,' Darcy said, appearing alongside.

'Let's go there.'

With the cold weather, the little bar was doing good business because a lot of people had turned up and wanted to see what was happening. Misset was among them, knocking back a *café fine*. He slunk out as he saw Pel. Despite his stealth, Pel didn't fail to spot him.

Coffee and brandy appeared. Darcy tried to pay but the proprietor waved the offer aside.

'Who do they claim to be?' Pel asked. 'Terrorists?'

'Plain villains, I think,' the Chief said. He looked as if he were about to explode. He was a big man who, although he was good at his job, tended to favour a bull-in-a-china-shop approach. 'The concierge next door thinks they got in during the night so we feel that's when the job started and it dragged on longer than expected. The first of the staff to arrive is Labarre, the under-manager. He opens up and he's always early. We think they didn't know that and intended to be away before anyone appeared. When he turned up there was only one thing they could do and that was take him hostage. After that, they had to take the others hostage too. They got them all except one of the secretaries, who arrived late.'

Pel frowned. 'It doesn't seem right somehow,' he said. 'You'd have thought with a job this big they'd have thought ahead a bit. How were they intending to get into the vaults?'

'They must have smuggled in cutting equipment.'

'How?'

Turgot appeared. His nose was red from the wind and he looked on edge, his mouth tight, his face drawn. 'We've got every spare man we have here,' he said. 'Next door. On the roof. In the buildings opposite. Everybody's armed and we have sharpshooters placed. Crack shots are due to arrive from Marseilles.'

'They ought to know what to do,' the Chief said.

'The men on the roof have got into the building through the top-storey windows,' Turgot said. 'Everything in the armoury's here. Telescopic sights. Rifles. Sub-machine guns. Tear gas. Stun grenades. They can't possibly get away.'

'Have you made contact?' Pel asked.

'Yes. They're demanding getaway cars, a safe passage to the airport, a plane and a ransom of a million for the manager, Gilbaud. They say they'll take him with them to ensure their getaway. If the ransom doesn't appear he'll be dumped – dead.'

'We picked up an abandoned car,' Pomereu of Traffic put in. 'It might have been intended as the getaway car. It was standing in the Rue Doctor-Chaveau. It was unlocked and pointing towards the Rue de la Liberté. It would be a good place for it. Fingerprints are going over it now.'

'How did they get in?'

'They must have acquired a key.'

'Which makes it an inside job. What else?'

'There are seven customers in there. They arrived before the manager and they had to hold them, too.'

'That makes twenty-three. How many villains?'

'We've learned now there are six.'

'A lot to crowd with the loot into a single getaway car. Could the car be a feint?'

The Chief looked quickly at Pel. Trust Pel to think of the unexpected. 'A feint?' he said.

'Perhaps they're not going to use it at all.'

Darcy produced his xeroxed copy of the diagram found in Meluc's wallet. By this time it was beginning to look a little dog-eared from all the handling it had had.

He laid it on the table in front of the Chief. The Chief glared at it. 'It doesn't seem to mean anything,' he growled.

'It must mean something,' Pel said. 'Today's date's on it. It must be part of this affair at the Crédit Rural.'

'Well, what?'

'Wiring? No alarms have gone off.'

'It doesn't look like a diagram of any wiring I can imagine,' Darcy said.

They argued round the diagram for a few minutes but none of them could suggest anything useful.

Eventually, it was Pel who brought them back to the facts.

'Anybody hurt so far?' he asked.

'One of the staff tried to break away,' Turgot said. 'He was hit with an iron bar. He's an old man, due for retirement – a brave old boy by the sound of him. He's now unconscious. There's a doctor in there, though. He was one of the customers who were trapped.'

'How did we learn all this? From the telephone?'

'It's still open.'

'How much money is involved?'

'The girl who was late is the manager's secretary. Name of Didon. Annette Didon. She'd been attending to her mother who'd had a fall and she had to get a doctor. She says around sixty to seventy million francs.'

'They won't give that up without a struggle. So it makes them dangerous.'

'We're facing ruthless men,' Turgot agreed. 'We're keeping the Didon girl here. She's in an office round the corner.She's a hard-headed type and not the sort to be hysterical. She's given us the names of all the bank staff and she's telling all she knows about the premises. We've got an architect with her, drawing a rough plan for us to work from. They can't get away.'

'They're obviously going to try,' the Chief remarked. 'If they're demanding a safe passage to the airport.'

'Has anything been done about that?' Pel asked.

'We've told them we'll try to arrange it,' the Chief said.

'Will we?'

'No.'

'Then hadn't we better make it seem that we will? If the telephone's open hadn't we better get the airport to ring the bank and tell them there's an executive jet available with a flight plan already filed? Something like that. If

41

they think they're going to get away with it, they may drop their guard a bit.'

The Chief looked at Turgot. 'Fix it,' he said.

'And', Pel added, 'a car parked handily in the square where they can see it. Then we can tell them everything's arranged for them.'

The Chief nodded. 'Have it done,' he told Turgot. He frowned. 'Well, that's the situation. We've set up a telephone exchange in the basement of the office next door. We've cleared both sides and nobody else's in the building at all except the concierge who might be needed. We've also got men in the apartments opposite and one or two in cars and vans about the square. We've got the whole of the front covered.'

'Sides?'

'Covered. If they try to dig their way through the walls, we'll be waiting.'

'Back?'

'Opens on to a yard with a gate that leads to an alley,' Turgot said. 'It pushes through to the Place St Bénigne. We have men there. They won't get out that way. We've also clamped microphones to the adjoining walls and we have men listening out. The reception's poor because the office where everybody's being held has a corridor on either side. We can hear talking but only from time to time as they go into the corridors. We can't perform miracles. It'll be better when the men above get their equipment in. They're trying to lower cameras and microphones to listen to what they're up to. They've threatened to shoot the manager in four hours' time and after that someone every hour.'

The Chief looked ferocious. 'There are innocent people in there,' he snapped.

'Can anything be done from underneath?'

'The whole area underneath is the bank vault. Surrounded by reinforced concrete. To get at them through there would require a job as big as the Channel Tunnel.'

Darcy joined in. 'They must be new boys,' he said. 'Or up from Marseilles. Everybody we have on *our* list is either in gaol or about to be. We've been pretty successful just lately.'

'We caught the name "Jacquot",' Turgot said. 'Ring a bell?'

It didn't.

'It would *have* to include a local boy or two,' Pel said. 'They'd need to know their way about to get away cleanly.'

'It looks like that,' Darcy agreed. 'This is a pretty complicated area of streets. With the main road blocked off they've got to go through the St Philibert district.'

Everybody knew the St Philibert area. It was one of the oldest parts of the city, a district of sagging roofs, sway-backed walls and unbelievably narrow streets.

Turgot looked worn out already. God knew what he'd look like before the affair was over. Pel's eyes caught Darcy's. Their place wasn't here at the site of the seige. With every uniformed cop in the city concentrated round the Church of St Philibert, somebody ought to be at the Hôtel de Police to look after the shop. After all, Pel was supposed to be the Chief's deputy and a siege wasn't really his affair at the moment.

As they left the press arrived. Sarrazin, the freelance, as usual acted as spokesman. 'What's happened, Chief?' he asked.

'What's it look like? It's a bank hold-up.'

'Guns?' Henriot of *Le Bien Public*, the local rag, asked. 'We've been told shots were fired.'

'They were. But not at anybody. Just warnings. There are sixteen staff in there and seven customers. They're being held hostages. They're demanding a car to take them to the airport and a plane to get them out of the country.'

'Will they get them?'

'I can hardly discuss that with you.'

'Okay, Chief. What else?'

'How much do you want?'

'Who's running the show?'

'The Chief.'

Sarrazin made a note on the back of a newspaper. 'Will he talk to us?'

'I think he's more likely to clap you in gaol just now. If I were you I'd keep out of his way. Stick to what you've got, which is about as much as we know. Confine yourselves to eye witnesses and your powers of imagination. You've got plenty of that, as I've noticed from past fairy stories you've written.'

Sarrazin grinned and they went off satisfied, the cogs and wheels in their brains whirring as their ideas took hold.

'We'll check the staff and their friends,' Pel said to Darcy as they prepared to head for their cars. 'After that, all we can do is wait and see what happens. If they get away with it – '

'They won't,' Turgot said dramatically. 'Never.'

Pel thought it unwise to count your chickens before they were hatched. A lot could happen – and often did.

'If they get away with it,' he repeated, 'that's when I'll be interested.'

4

At just about the time the police were taking the first steps towards solving the identities of the bank robbers, a girl was sitting painting in one of the long galleries of the Musée des Arts Modernes in the Rue Lacoste near the University.

The Musée des Arts Modernes was not a big place and its director was Arthur Leygues. The building belonged to the city, as did many of the exhibits, but there were also many privately owned exhibits belonging to Leygues himself. He had inherited an enormous fortune from his father who had made it from chemicals, but he also had a degree from the Sorbonne in art and history and some skill of his own as a painter. He had started off by opening a small gallery in Paris, but he wasn't very interested in the buying and selling of pictures, preferring simply to show them.

By offering his own collection and agreeing to act as curator, he had approached the City Fathers with the suggestion that they use the Château de Nohailles near the University as their new museum. The château had once been in the country but the sprawl of a modern city and the expansion of the University had engulfed it so that, in the end, it had proved to be in a perfect position for a museum. The City Fathers had agreed to Leygues' proposal and he had happily moved his personal collection into the château. Grants and gifts had enabled him to enlarge the collection until it was now not only quite extensive but also well balanced and valuable. In one quiet corner where it was hardly noticed Leygues had placed a modest example of his own work. The suggestion that he should do so had come from the City Fathers, as much as anything to indicate to visitors that the director at least knew what he was talking about.

The 1900 Room was on the second floor of the building. The light was good, coming as it did from long windows that looked over the better, greener half of the city. At one side of the room two pictures rested on easels – one a Douanier Rousseau of a woodland scene with green, yellow and red trees in the background under a cloudy sky; the other a Gustave Paot, an artist of no great note until recent years but a Burgundian who had painted in and around the city. The prices for his works had been creeping steadily up and when one of them had unexpectedly fetched half a million francs in London his name was made. Douanier Rousseau's paintings were already of great value.

The two paintings had been removed from their frames. They were quite small – both about sixty by forty centimetres. Alongside them were two other easels bearing what appeared to be identical paintings. The girl who worked on the copies was tall, beautiful and surprisingly elegant, even in her paint-stained smock. The uniformed *gardien*, who sat on a chair in the doorway, smiled at her with affection. She had been working on the copies for some time now and he had got to know her well. His job was to watch the gallery like a hawk. Other *gardiens* sat in the doorways of other rooms and galleries. Marc Distaing considered himself lucky. He liked the paintings in the 1900 Room – Rousseaus, Utrillos, a Chagall, a Bernier, two Bonnards and the vivid Paot. The Paot was similar in style to the Rousseaus but it was the colours that hit you in the eye – reds, yellows, blues, all the

46

primary colours, with a whole host of others that literally dazzled. Distaing loved the Paot.

The girl's name was Colette Esterhazy and she was taking a degree in History of Art at the University, keeping herself at the same time by doing occasional painting commissions. Distaing considered her good enough to need no degree and quite beautiful enough to be her own model. She had taken instruction from Arthur Leygues himself and, Distaing believed, had become his mistress. Distaing couldn't imagine Leygues allowing pictures to be taken from their frames for any other reason.

The girl started to put her things together and clean her brushes.

'Don't you find it hard work painting two at once?' Distaing asked.

'No. And it saves time. They're similar in style and colours and it's easy to switch from one to the other. While one dries, I work on the other. Monsieur Leygues is very happy about it.'

'What'll you do with them when you've finished them?'

'They're to be part of my degree course. I think two paintings like these speak for themselves. They'll carry far more weight than a long essay.'

Distaing nodded enthusiastically and was treated to a smile. He wished he were younger, had a lot of money and owned a picture gallery. Apart from the fact that Arthur Leygues was a lot older than he was, he even wouldn't have minded being Arthur Leygues.

'Time to lock up,' he said. It was his duty to walk round the gallery checking everything and switching on the alarms before he went off duty but, as he'd been there all day watching the beautiful Colette Esterhazy, his inspection was a casual one.

'When do you take them away?' he asked.

'Now,' she said. 'They're finished. I've just been touching them up. They'll be dry in no time.'

As she gathered her belongings together the telephone at the end of the gallery rang and Distaing answered a query about the Douanier Rousseau. It came from a man who said he was speaking for Editions Lafayette, a Paris publisher who was producing a coffee-table edition of turn-of-the-century paintings. He was wondering if he could get permission to reproduce.

Distaing knew Editions Lafayette well. 'You'd have to ask Monsieur Leygues,' he said. 'It's nothing to do with me.'

'Of course. I realize that. I'm just checking that you're displaying. I asked them to put me through to you. I want to know about the Rousseaus you have.'

'We have two. *Bois de Boulogne* and *Scene Near Enghien*.'

'Ah, that's what I wanted to know. We'd misplaced the *Scene Near Enghien*. We'd placed it in Aix. It's a wonderful painting, that, isn't it?'

The caller sounded enthusiastic and kept Distaing chatting for a good five minutes. Distaing didn't mind. He enjoyed talking about the paintings under his care and there was no one in the gallery. Only Colette Esterhazy.

As he put the telephone down, he saw her coming towards him. She carried the paintings – squares of canvas on wooden stretchers – one in each hand. Her equipment was in a huge sling bag on her back.

'Good-night,' she said cheerfully.

'Finished?' Distaing was disappointed.

'Only for the time being. I shall be back again in the autumn. Monsieur Leygues says I can come any time. I've only to ask and he'll get whatever I want put on an easel.'

'Will you sell them eventually?'

'Why not? Pity they don't pay the real prices for them. Good-night, Monsieur Distaing.'

'Good-night, mademoiselle. I'll look forward to seeing you again.'

The gallery was empty so he walked with her to the staircase and stood watching her as she tripped down. A car was waiting outside. As the door closed behind her, he heard the engine start and the car draw away at speed.

Uplifted a little by his chat with a beautiful girl, Distaing walked back to his position by the door of the gallery. The two pictures still stood on their easels glowing in the light that came from the windows. Despite his loyalty to the great masters, Distaing considered it a bit silly that a painting and an exact copy of that painting, treated with loving care, every brush stroke counting, every nuance of style taken into consideration, should have different values. Surely to God, he felt, they were the same thing. The only difference was that one was painted a century before by a name that had become famous, the other by a girl who was twice as beautiful and probably just as skilful. It was a matter of inspiration and original thought, he supposed.

He imagined his job the following day would be to return the paintings to their frames and the frames to their places on the wall. He went to them and studied them. He enjoyed looking at them. Funny, though, he thought, old Douanier Rousseau, the customs official turned painter, sometimes got his colours not quite the same. On this one, there was a touch of red on one of the background trees that seemed to jar.

Distaing peered a little more closely. Then he reached out his finger. The paint in the corner was still tacky. He straightened up, frowning, his mind working slowly. If the paint on this one was tacky, he thought, then the one that had been carried out of the museum by Colette

Esterhazy must have been dry. And if that painting were dry, then the one on the easel which was still tacky must be the copy. In which case the one the girl had carried out of the museum must be –

'Name of God,' he yelled. 'She switched the pictures.'

The news of the theft hit the Hôtel de Police just as Pel and Darcy were organizing their forces for the hostage situation at the Banque Crédit Rural. The siege wasn't their baby but they were already involved because the sooner they could establish the identity of the robbers the easier it would be.

Pel looked up as Annie Saxe brought the news. He frowned, thinking bitterly how inconsiderate it was of villains to commit two crimes one on top of another. The police already had enough on their plate with the Crédit Rural job.

'Get Nosjean,' he snapped irritatedly. 'Tell him to handle it.'

Nosjean always got the art jobs these days because he shared a flat with Marie-Josephine Lehmann, known as Mijo, who worked at the University and knew more about art than anyone they knew. She had helped the police on more than one occasion so that whenever anything like this came up they used Nosjean and he flew to her at once.

When he appeared in her office, she emerged from behind the piles of art books that stood on her desk and hooted with laughter.

'It's the oldest dodge in the art business,' she said. 'Copy a painting and at the last minute switch them to take away the real one and leave the copy. It's been done before and it'll be done again.'

'Isn't it a bit silly to *allow* people to copy masterpieces?' Nosjean asked.

She kissed him. 'You've a lot to learn, *mon brave*,' she said. 'All galleries have people copying their paintings. You can go round the Uffizi and the Pitti galleries in Florence and find people making perfect copies of people like Barbari or Tintoretto, even Botticelli. Sometimes you can hardly tell the difference.'

'Isn't it dangerous?'

'Mostly it isn't, because the people are known to the owner of the gallery. They're usually students. Scholarship in art requires knowledge of the methods of the old masters and the best way to acquire that surely is to copy them, brush stroke by brush stroke.'

'What will she do with them?'

Mijo shrugged. 'There are various ways of handling a stolen picture. She could sell it at once, for instance, and make a profit. Or she could keep it and copy it several times and make a *bigger* profit. But that requires work and concentration and mostly they prefer to get rid of them quickly and vanish. When Canaletto's *View of Venice* was stolen they copied it so many times word got around that dealers were growing suspicious so they stopped and got out of it and looked for another. Perhaps this is it. All we have to do is put the word round the dealers. I'll do it for you.'

'Where will she be?'

'Depends on what she intends. If she's intending to copy she'll disappear somewhere she can't be found and the copies will be sold. In the States. South America. Canada. Japan. Places as far away as possible from the source of the original. There'll be a little provenance. But not much. Just enough to whet the appetites of the prospective buyers who'll want to believe they've bought a lost Rousseau or a lost Paot.'

'What will they pay for them?'

'A lot. When they've sold them all they'll have done very well indeed. You'll probably find the museum will wake up one day to find the originals on their doorstep. When the *Mona Lisa* was stolen from the Louvre, it was returned unharmed but by that time there were a dozen copies believed to be floating around in private collections across the world.'

'Surely the people who bought them realized they were fakes when the original was returned?'

'Did they? They weren't even sure that the one that was returned was the original. And the buyers would never admit receiving a stolen painting.'

As Nosjean had discovered before, the art world was a curious one with more mysteries in it than facts.

Mijo paused. 'This time,' she went on slowly, 'I have a feeling they'll disappear abroad.'

'Why do you feel that?'

'Just a hunch. There've been so many things appearing lately the market's tightened up. Some type stole a Tiepolo from the Academy of Fine Arts in Venice a little while ago and had to post it back because he couldn't sell it. People have become wary. A lot of last-century rubbish is being offered these days as masterpieces. Your paintings will end up looking like last-century rubbish.'

'Can they be disguised that easily?'

'Of course. You paint them over with acrylic. It's easy to put on and just as easy to take off. They'll look like two more examples of last-century rubbish that will bring in just enough to be worth exporting but not enough to be worth investigating.'

Nosjean was still puzzled. 'How did she get permission to have the paintings removed from the frames?'

Mijo's view was the same as Distaing's. 'Have a guess,' she said.

Leygues was in the States buying. He had been telephoned and was already on his way back, and it was left to his deputy, a man called Lepic, to meet Nosjean.

He was a small man with spectacles and he was distraught. 'It should never have been allowed,' he insisted. 'I said so. More than once. Copying's always permitted. But to take the paintings from their frames and place them on easels was asking for trouble. They would be very light and easy to carry. And two.' His voice rose. 'Not just one. Two.'

'Why was it allowed in this case?' Nosjean asked.

Lepic shrugged and flapped his hands. 'I can only think it was because this girl, Colette Esterhazy, is pretty.' He paused. 'No,' he went on, 'she's more than pretty. She's beautiful. I believe she's modelled for artists. She's very, very beautiful and very, very clever. I think there was a man behind her.'

'Who gave this permission?'

'Monsieur Leygues.'

'Was this usual?'

'No.'

'Then why this time?'

Lepic flapped his hands again. 'I suspect', he said discreetly, 'that Monsieur Leygues was more than normally attracted to the girl.'

'This telephone call that came?'

'It was said to be from Editions Lafayette in Paris. They've contacted us before. Occasionally they come with their cameras to photograph a painting for publication. They've worked for us, producing prints, pamphlets and booklets which we sell at the museum shop.' Lepic fished among the papers on his desk and pushed across a book. It was large and in full colour. He riffled through the pages and indicated an illustration. 'That's the Rousseau.' Another page turned. 'That's the Paot. Lafeyette also take pictures for their own use, for which they pay us a royalty, of course. Whoever made the call

53

convinced the staff that it was genuine. They insiste d on talking to Distaing, the *gardien*. This we allow. The *gardien*s acquire a surprising amount of knowledge about the paintings they watch over. Distaing's particularly good. But it was nothing but a sham, to draw his attention away while the girl switched the pictures.'

'I think I'd better talk to Distaing.'

Distaing was still a bit upset by what had happened. 'She'd been so often before.' he said. 'She was here in the summer copying a Picasso. She said it was for her degree.'

'How many paintings did she need for her degree?'

'I don't know. It was nothing to do with me. Monsieur Leygues told me to take the pictures down and remove the frames and stick them on easels for her. That's what I did.'

'What about this telephone call that came?'

'It must have been an accomplice. He kept me talking a long time.'

'So you weren't watching her *all the time*?'

'I took my eyes off her only while I was answering the telephone. It was at the far end of the gallery and there was a piece by Rodin between me and her. But I wasn't worried. She'd been in the gallery so often – and with permission from the top brass – she was almost part of the fittings. When I returned from the telephone, she was on her way out. It was only after she'd gone that I examined the pictures on the easels. They were the ones she'd been working on. The originals had gone.'

'You went with her to the stairs, I believe.'

'Yes.'

'Why?'

Distaing looked sheepish. 'Well,' he said, 'because . . . well . . . well, just because she was so beautiful, I suppose. You don't see faces and figures like she has all that often. I like art myself. But I prefer it in the flesh. If I had a daughter who looked like that I wouldn't rest till I'd got her married off.'

Nosjean studied him. Could the man behind Colette Esterhazy be Distaing? He was young enough to be attracted to her. He knew how the museum was run. But there had been someone else, someone waiting with a car. According to Distaing, she had got into the car and it had driven off immediately. So who *was* this man? It must have been a man. Nosjean's experience told him it wasn't another girl. It had all the hallmarks of a man who had got a naïve girl under his influence.

It seemed a good idea before he did anything else for Nosjean to see if Colette Esterhazy was at home. He might – though he very much doubted it – just catch her before she vanished into the blue.

She lived in a block of flats owned by a Madame Sadon in which she had rented the top one. It had a skylight that whispered under a shower of rain as Nosjean stepped inside. There were one or two canvases lying about, but nothing that had been finished, and there were no personal belongings.

'She took it because she said the light was good,' Madame Sadon said. 'She painted a lot. Sometimes a man called Courtrand came and painted her, using her easel and materials. She posed for him.' Her lips pursed. 'In the nude,' she added. 'What else they got up to, I don't know.'

'What about other men?'

'One or two. From the University. My daughter's there. She knew them.'

The daughter, a mousy girl called Eloise, was willing to talk.

'She was so beautiful,' she said in a breathless whisper. 'She was like a film star. A bit like Catherine Deneuve but taller. She was wonderful. I thought the world of her. She was always so kind to me and it wasn't because I'm beautiful and brilliant because I'm not and I know it.'

She was plump and unattractive but it was clear she had had a heavy crush on Colette Esterhazy who, in addition to being beautiful and easygoing and happy, was also, it seemed, unfailingly kind to girls less fortunate than she was. It was something that didn't often happen with beautiful girls, Nosjean knew. He had suffered in his youth from beautiful girls who had been cruel enough to jeer at his habit of blushing and his general unhandiness as a courtier.

'When did she leave?' he asked.

The girl shrugged. 'No one saw her go,' she said. 'She must have gone straight off from the museum. I think she moved most of her belongings the day before without us knowing. She looked after herself so we didn't go into her room. She left a note. It said there were some things she didn't want that I could have.'

'What sort of things?'

'Clothes. They were beautiful. She was kind enough to think of me even then.'

Eloise gave Nosjean a sickly grin and he left hurriedly.

5

At the Crédit Rural nothing happened. Nobody had
expected much to happen but the fact that it didn't left
them angry and frustrated. The thought that six men in
the Banque Crédit Rural were holding a city to ransom
was infuriating but there was little the police could do
about it. It was policy to do nothing and it was a policy
with which Pel was in complete agreement. Criminals
were too often hyped up with booze or drugs or by the
sheer exhilaration of being criminals, and it was an emotion that faded quickly when the exploit they'd planned
unexpectedly died away into a dull and tedious exercise.
Criminals weren't always good at being patient.

'They want drinks sent in,' Turgot reported.

The Chief, who by this time was becoming speechless
with anger, merely waved and the drinks were placed
outside the door of the bank. The door opened and the
drinks vanished inside.

'Can't we rush them?' Turgot asked in desperation.
'Next time they ask for anything and open the door,
can't we have a squad ready to batter the door wide
open?'

'And have the hostages shot?' the Chief asked.

The sharpshooters arrived from Lyons and began to
throw their weight about, demanding the best positions.
They were followed by a squad from the Search, Assist,
Intervene and Dissuade Brigade, who were normally

used against terrorists and whom the Chief had been grudgingly forced to call in.

'Paris insisted,' he said witheringly.

Since the bank was virtually in the centre of the city, the traffic snarl-up was tremendous. It lasted all through the morning until Traffic succeeded in devising a deviation round the area. Busy over his Plan-Guide Blay, Inspector Pomereu, whose job it was, could be heard muttering to himself, 'Rue de l'Arquebuse' or 'Boulevard de Sévigné' or 'Rue de la Liberté' until finally he handed the list of street names he had decided on to his deputy.

'That's it,' he said. 'Get it organized. Get a city street map xeroxed and marked out. Yellow marker along the streets we're using. The Chief will want a copy. So will Pel and Turgot. It might have to be changed here and there if it doesn't work but that will do for the time being.'

'It'll be hell,' his deputy observed.

'Aren't all deviations?' Pomereu said.

As he turned away, his men went out with barriers and signs and posted traffic cops, and the snarled-up traffic slowly began to move. Turgot was still in touch with the spokesman for the bank robbers. He was uncertain what to do next.

'Wait,' Pel advised. 'Just wait.'

In the streets around, there were dozens of would-be spectators, kept from close proximity to the scene by the police. Most of those who had been there at the beginning had long since wandered off, but new ones had arrived, together with many small boys caught by the excitement. Pierre la Poche, only recently out of 72, Rue d'Auxonne, by which name the local gaol was known, was among those who had seen the possibilities of the situation. He had been picked up with his hand in a spectator's back pocket, and a woman's handbag had been snatched. There were opportunities everywhere if you only looked for them.

As the afternoon arrived they were still waiting. Turgot had been in touch with the men in the bank again. 'They haven't changed their demands,' he said as Pel appeared beside him. 'They're still insisting on a car to the airport with a plane standing by.'

'They've left it too late,' Pel observed. 'Where are they intending to go?'

'Romania's been suggested.'

'Well, perhaps they deserve each other.'

'They're still threatening to shoot the manager.'

'They said that early this morning. They haven't done it yet.'

The telephone that had been linked to a line into the bank shrilled and Turgot snatched it up. Pel and the Chief listened on the extensions.

'We haven't changed our minds,' said the heavily disguised voice at the other end of the line. 'We're still waiting.'

Pel wondered if the caller was talking into a handkerchief or into a box of some kind. His voice was certainly effectively muffled.

'Send out the women,' Turgot insisted.

'We'll think about it,' replied Pel, unwilling to commit himself at least for the moment.

A psychiatrist was brought to the scene to see if he could suggest a new approach. Pel observed with irony that he was thin and wild-eyed and looked as though he were badly in need of psychiatric help himself. But he talked to the crooks and then returned to announce they were in a no-win situation and were desperate.

'Name of God, we know that,' the Chief snapped.

'They're living off excitement,' the psychiatrist confided earnestly. 'It's something we've learned from examinations.'

The Chief glared at him. 'Holy Mother of God,' he snarled, 'policemen learn that within the first month of their service. *Without the benefit of psychoanalysis.*'

The psychiatrist didn't last long.

The CRS men began to demand action. They'd been sent there to provide action, they said. They were cold and they couldn't see any sense in just sitting around. They were armed with stun grenades and every one of them was trained for such a situation.

'No,' the Chief said. He had calmed down a lot in the hours since he'd first been called out. 'There are women in there.'

'We can take those guys out.'

'And a few others with them,' the Chief snapped. 'I know you lot. Once you get started you take a lot of stopping.'

The snipers thought they could pick off the robbers if they could only get them to the window.

'Lined up?' the Chief snarled. 'Like targets on a fairground stall? You'd only need to hit one and the rest would go berserk.'

As the snipers' leader moved away, the Chief turned to Pel. 'What would you do?' he asked.

'Wait,' said Pel gloomily. 'And keep on waiting.'

The day continued to drag. It had started off gloomy with winter threatening and a line of heavy cloud that looked like snow hanging over the hills to the north. The sun had come out around midday, the first rays touching the varnished roofs for which the city was famous. It caught the spires of the city's churches – Notre Dame, St Michel, St Jean, St Philibert, Ste Odile, Sacré Coeur and a few others – and coloured the high roofs of the Palais des Ducs, the Porte Guillaume and the Place de la Libération. The light splashed off the curves of cars moving round the University and the Industrial Zone and down the Cours de Gaulle. Having given a spectacular display the sun then vanished abruptly. There was no mistaking the message. It wasn't yet winter but everybody knew it was right on the doorstep.

During the afternoon the weather changed back to rain. On the roofs round the Crédit Rural, the policemen on watch turned their collars up and tried to find enough shelter to allow themselves to keep their eye on the ball. Turgot began to worry that rain would blur the view and spoil the sharpshooters' aim if it came to shooting.

The light faded quickly, the day becoming grey and wet so that the queues of homegoing shoppers scrambled thankfully aboard the buses, glad to be out of the rain. The streams of cars beginning to make their way from the city centre to the suburbs, their wheels throwing up a mist of water from the wet road, had their windscreen wipers going, the glass reflecting the kaleidoscope of the neon signs and the red, yellow and green of the traffic lights. In the Rue de la Queste still nothing moved.

Afternoon crawled towards evening and the CRS men again suggested that they should go in. But, like the ever-cautious Pel, the Chief was still for waiting and as the light began to go he sent for illumination.

At just about the time when the police were setting up screens and hauling stands bearing arc lights into position in preparation for an all-night siege, they unexpectedly discovered the meaning of the strange ray-like diagram that had been found in Robert Meluc's pocket.

Oddly enough, it was Misset, of all people, who realized it first whilst studying the xerox of the strange-shaped diagram as he sat by the telephone. Alongside him was a copy of the plan prepared by Inspector Pomereu to indicate to Pel's department just where the traffic deviations ran, where the barriers had been raised. To keep traffic away from the bank and to enable the police to conduct their operations without hindrance, roads had been sealed off and office workers and shoppers were having to do their business outside that area. Buses were going round a perimeter consisting of the Rue de l'Arquebuse, the Boulevard de Sévigné, the Rue de la Liberté, the Rue Bossuet and the Rue Monge. Smaller roads were also involved, where buses and vans were scraping their way past with difficulty, hemmed in by honking cars, but those were the main thoroughfares affected. In addition to keeping the traffic moving, the deviations and the sealing of roads meant that if the men in the Crédit Rural decided to bolt, they would find the main roads out of the city already cut off.

Misset wasn't a man whose brain was very active. It wasn't that he was stupid. He saw things when they appeared in front of him brightly lit and sounding a warning. It was just that he had lost most of his ambition, and for most of the time kept his brain in neutral. But now, as he stared at the xeroxed diagram and the route Pomereu had drawn up for the deviations round the Rue de la Queste, he suddenly noticed that they matched each other like the image in a mirror reflecting its subject. Turning the diagram Doc Minet had found upside down, he realized it was almost the same as Pomereu's route. Without any indication about which was top and which was bottom they had been misled by the hurriedly scrawled date and had been looking at it upside down. Now, studying it the right way up, he saw they were remarkably similar. Not exactly alike, but Pomereu's routes seemed to follow the lines of the diagram.

Finding a piece of tracing paper – not without difficulty – he traced the route Pomereu had drawn. It had been taken from the city map in the Plan-Guide Blay and it fitted almost exactly over the diagram found on Robert Meluc.

Misset could hardly contain his excitement. Reaching for the radio telephone, he got in touch with the operational headquarters of the men surrounding the Crédit Rural in the back room of the Café St Michel. This, he thought wildly, would ensure promotion and for the first time in years ambition touched him and he saw himself being advanced in rank, even saw himself eventually sitting in the Chief's chair. The fantasy was pleasant but eventually unsustaining.

Unhappily for Misset, he was just too late. At about the time he was trying to get in touch, an old man, Richard Bridier, was walking his dog in the Place Nozay. It was a brown miniature poodle called Tou-Tou. It was suffering from a form of eczema and, like its owner, was getting on in years. Bridier lived in a second-floor apartment in the Rue Saules, behind the Church of St Philibert, and the dog had belonged to his wife. She had died the previous year and the dog was now his sole companion: his only child had emigrated to Canada years before and never bothered to write.

The dog had been fidgeting and whining for some time and the situation had begun to be tricky for Bridier hadn't wanted to go out at all with the tension in the street. But, grimly, he knew he had no other option and, taking the lead, he lifted the dog to the crook of his arm and headed for the stairs.

'Let's go, Tou-Tou,' he said. 'Come on, old boy.'

Near the church Bridier could see groups of people and police with rifles and, deciding that his route might be dangerous, he turned in the opposite direction. From the Rue Saules he arrived in the Rue Croix Moreaud which led him into the Place Nozay which was virtually empty. It had been cut off so well by the traffic deviations that some of the shops hadn't even bothered to open. It seemed perfect for the dog.

He put Tou-Tou down and slipped the lead. Immediately the dog cocked its leg against a tree with a look of ecstasy. Having completed the task, Tou-Tou wandered over to a manhole cover where he stopped and sniffed, looking more than usually interested.

'What is it, little one?' Bridier asked. 'Something interesting?'

He always talked to the dog who never took any notice. Probably Tou-Tou thought him a silly old fool with his baby talk.

Then to Bridier's surprise, the manhole cover moved and he froze. It slowly lifted and a man emerged. He was dressed in overalls and wore an orange protective helmet. There were marks on his sleeve as if he had brushed against a damp and dirty wall. In his hand he carried a large canvas sack. He looked at Bridier and climbed through the manhole to the street. Behind him a second man appeared, similarly dressed. Then a third and a fourth and a fifth and a sixth. They were all dressed in similar fashion and they carried large canvas holdalls. Under Bridier's startled gaze, the last one carefully replaced the manhole cover and then, turning to Bridier, courteously raised his helmet, gave a little bow, and walked away after the others.

Across the square, pointing away from the restricted streets towards the free access to the rest of the city, was a large, dark blue builder's van into which the six men climbed. Then the engine started and the van roared away. Bridier stared after it, unable to understand what had happened. He had seen men at work in manholes before, repairing electricity mains or gas mains or water mains. But never so many – not such unlikely looking labourers.

When Pel returned to the Crédit Rural the whole area around had come to a standstill. A security van was parked nearby which had arrived during the afternoon and Turgot's squad were still questioning the crew. 'We might find out who knew they were coming,' he said. 'Today's clearance day when the old notes are replaced by new ones and we're going to have a job identifying the ones they take if they get away.

'We've now heard', he went on, 'that the old boy who collapsed – name of Malabry, Jules Malabry – has died without recovering consciousness. Doc Minet says it must have been a heart attack brought on by the blow he received.'

'Well, that's the first casualty,' Pel remarked wearily.

'There might be a lot more before this is over,' said Turgot sadly. 'They seem pretty determined. We've emptied the districts of men to screen the Rue de la Queste area. I've asked for more. They've still got the manager and the under-manager and they swear they'll shoot them if we don't let them go.'

'We've promised them everything they want,' the Chief snarled. 'Why don't they come out?'

'They don't believe you'll keep your promises,' Pel said drily.

'I won't,' the Chief snapped. 'I don't bargain with crooks and terrorists. As soon as they stick their noses out of the door, they're ours.'

'They'll have hostages,' Pel warned him unnecessarily.

'Since the bombing last year, there's been a barrier at the airport and they don't seem to have thought of that,' snarled the Chief. 'They'll have to stop and that's when we'll get them. We have men there,' he added smugly.

Pel frowned. 'There's something odd about this business,' he said thoughtfully. 'For ruthless men prepared to murder, they've become remarkably quiet. And if there's an insider who gave them information, why didn't they know the under-manager always arrived early? Are we still in touch?'

'They haven't had anything to say for some time,' Turgot pointed out with sudden unease. 'The last time they demanded food.'

'Caviare? Turbot? Coq au vin?'

The Chief glared. 'They get nothing more from me,' he growled. 'How long since they were in contact?'

'Nearly two hours. I suppose they're working things out.'

'Perhaps they've worked them out,' Pel said cryptically.

The Chief was just trying to sort out what he meant when Sergeant Lotier, Turgot's deputy, pushed his head round the door.

'Something's happening,' he said. 'The man with the headphones reports women talking.'

'Women? Are they free?'

'We can also see movement behind the window,' he added bleakly.

In sudden agitation they hurried outside and watched from behind a police van. The windows of the bank were of opaque glass but there was definitely movement. Then, quite clearly beyond the glass, they saw the shape of a man who seemed to be struggling at the window.

'Get the Didon girl,' the Chief rapped.

Annette Didon appeared within a minute or two. She was a tall attractive woman in her late twenties. She stared at the blurred figure beyond the glass. 'That's Monsieur Labarre,' she said. 'The under-manager. I recognize him.'

'Even through that glass?'

'Even through the glass.'

The Chief whirled. 'Get Turgot,' he roared. His eyes were glazed with shock and sudden realization.

As the Chief disappeared, looking urgently for some-one to demolish, Annie Saxe appeared. 'Patron,' she yelled at Pel. 'Misset called in. He says he's discovered what that ray-shaped thing was. It's the route of the deviations Traffic set up.'

'What?' Now it was the taciturn Pel's turn to panic.

'He says it was done from the Plan-Guide Blay map which matches Traffic's map almost exactly – but it's the other way up.'

'Who's got a map?'

Half a dozen Blay guides appeared immediately and, sure enough, Misset was right.

Pel stared at the map, the perspiration breaking out on his forehead. 'How in God's name did they know where Pomereu would place his deviations?' he snapped. 'And this tail thing. Where does that lead to? It appears to start around here in the Rue de la Queste . . .'

'And seems to stop somewhere round the Place No-zay,' Darcy said. 'It's a pity Misset didn't notice it before.'

'It's a pity', Pel said, 'that none of us did. Get over there, Daniel, and see what you can find out. Now.'

The Chief was sitting in the office of Gilbaud, the bank manager. He looked as if he were about to internally explode. By permission of Gilbaud, he was in the manager's chair while Gilbaud sat alongside him, thereby retaining his authority but allowing the Chief the position of supreme outraged importance. After a pre-liminary prowl round the premises, among scattered pieces of rope, paper and discarded clothing, the Chief had decided that it was his job to soothe the hostages. He had left the rest to his underlings, who were now poking into the various rooms and passages, trying to find out how the robbers had escaped without being seen. In a half-circle in front of him on chairs were the bank staff

and the seven frightened customers. They were surrounded by policemen, doctors and a psychiatrist from
the Hospital of the Sacred Heart. The body of the man
who had died of a heart attack had been removed and the
remaining survivors were suffering from nothing more
than the after-effects of being bound and gagged. There
was no sign of their captors and the Chief was trying to
ask his questions gently, fighting all the time to hold
down the lid on his explosive fury over their crafty
escape.

'How in the name of God did they get away?' he kept
asking feverishly.

The hostages weren't able to help much. They had
been obliged to lie face down on the floor, with their
hands tied behind their backs. They were all excited and
one or two of the women were touched by shock and on
the edge of hysteria. Those less affected by the ordeal
were answering questions. Only when they had seen no
movement for some time had the under-manager succeeded in struggling to the window to raise the alarm.
But they were all clear on one aspect. The raiders all had
weapons.

'Rifles?' Pel asked.

'No,' one of the typists said. 'Pistols. Or are they
revolvers? That sort of thing anyway. Like cowboys use.'

'No rifles,' Pel mused. 'Funny that people as desperate
as these seemed prepared to be would have nothing
more than hand guns.'

But apart from the man who had died from natural
causes, albeit brought on by a blow from a cosh, no one
was hurt. Not even the manager or the under-manager.
That was something. The ropes which had bound them
and the gags that had chafed their jaws lay on a desk to
be examined later in the hope they would produce some
clue to the identities of the thieves. The whole affair, Pel
considered, had been conducted coolly and the staff and

customers had been obliged to lie still while the gang, using the manager's keys, had opened the vault and removed safe deposit boxes. They had shared their spoils on the floor of the office and Bonds and similar documents had been tossed aside. Clearly they had been after only money or jewellery.

The police still hadn't worked out how the robbers had entered and left the premises, though at that moment Sergeant Lotier was beginning to get warm. Trampling through scattered paper, envelopes and forms, he was wondering why so much of the material that was normally in the stationery store-room was stacked neatly in the corridor and what advantage it could have been to the robbers.

He tried the door of the store-room. It was locked, but with a key borrowed from the manager's secretary he managed to open it. Inside he found himself staring at a wooden cupboard that took up a large proportion of the rear wall of the room. It was locked. He tried to pull it aside and was surprised to find it would move. He finally managed to shift it away from the wall and, after a moment or two of silent astonishment, he began to head to where the Chief was holding court.

At the same moment Darcy arrived back from the Place Nozay with the information that six men had been seen climbing out of a manhole there.

'What!' The Chief's voice rose to a shriek and the assembled company anticipated apoplexy.

Immediately, it had become clear what had happened. The gang had deliberately made the robbery appear to be a dangerous situation with hostages and as a result this had concentrated every available policeman in the city round the bank while the robbers had entered the sewers, strolled casually under the streets to the Place Nozay, five hundred metres away, and there emerged unnoticed, well behind the police cordon, a good hour before their escape had even been discovered. The Chief buried his head in his hands and gave up. He needed a drink. Several drinks.

6

The inquest into the robbery was held next day as hundreds of angry customers crammed into the bank demanding to know whether their safe deposit boxes containing savings and jewels were intact. 'A lot of them contained money,' the Chief told Pel. He looked grey and liverish. 'Cash. Stuck in there to hide it from tax inspectors, I expect. While we were negotiating with their spokesman, they were stuffing sacks with large-denomination used notes and cracking open safe deposit boxes. There were dozens in the vault and they'd got the key from Gilbaud.' His voice was sepulchral with gloom.

It was now becoming all too clear exactly what had occurred. A thirty-metre-long tunnel, dug from one of the sewers and out of sight of anything but a very careful inspection, had been discovered. The careful excavation ended up behind the bank's stationery store where all forms, documents, headed notepaper, envelopes, files, typewriter and word processor ribbons, and other paraphernalia were stored. The gang had made a hole in the wall big enough to climb through, and got into the bank that way. It had not occurred to Annette Didon in her description of the premises to mention the humble store-room.

'It must have taken several days to dig,' the Chief told them. 'It was driven from the sewer that leads from the Place Nozay – as a perfect escape route. Apart from the man who was there as they climbed from the manhole, nobody ever saw them.'

Pel reported that the van had been found at St Barien, north of the city, and the investigation had revealed certain interesting facts.

'It belongs to Meluc,' Darcy said, 'the guy found in the canal, and it's the vehicle that was missing. It would be just about right for six men and several sacks of loot. In addition to traces of cement, brick dust and plaster, the vehicle also contained two fifty-franc notes that had slipped under a broken tile.'

'There are dabs all over it,' Prélat, of Fingerprints, said. 'They're Meluc's. All the others are smudges. Our friends were wearing gloves. But this is the van they used all right, the one that old boy saw them climb into and drive away.'

The bank had immediately offered a substantial reward for anyone bringing in information that would lead to the arrest of the robbers. It was the usual procedure, even if it was done only to reassure their customers. The police put up another sum.

'It's big enough now to be tempting,' the Chief snarled. 'Somebody might nibble. The money's stashed away somewhere but it won't be easy to hide.'

'If I know the way their minds work,' Pel said thoughtfully, 'they won't touch it until the thing's blown over.'

Dressed in overalls and wearing a protective helmet, Pel wrinkled his nose with distaste as he descended with Darcy from the manhole in the Place Nozay. He looked like a cat on a wet pavement as he followed an inspector of sewers called Benoist along a narrow footway that ran alongside a channel of swiftly flowing water. But Pel was surprised to find the system cleaner than he had expected.

It was a strange echoing world down there, a land of waterfalls and hurrying rivers, the main sewer almost as wide as a railway tunnel, fed at intervals by streams from minor sewers carrying water from higher levels that had been cleansed in its fall. The air in the main sewer was surprisingly clear but everywhere there was the sound of rushing water.

Benoist then produced a plan which showed that it was easy to move underground from the Place Nozay where Bridier had seen the men emerge from the manhole to the Rue de la Queste where the bank was situated. When they turned off the main sewer, they began to find a scum of orange peel, twigs, cigarette packets, pieces of plastic, every kind of minor debris imaginable floating in the water caught in the angles of the channels. The smell deteriorated considerably here. After the fresher air of the main sewer it was unpleasant and Pel was sure he could hear rats.

Eventually they came to a sharp turn where the water swirled away in a rushing fall to a lower level. Reaching a small recess, Benoist led the way to the tunnel. Propped up alongside it was a sheet of plywood cut to fit the entrance and smeared with cement to look like part of the wall. 'They must have had it dug for some time,' Benoist said. 'And just plugged the end up with this until they were ready.' Pel nodded gloomily.

An army surplus field telephone lay on the walkway with a wire running down the tunnel to the bank which had been abandoned or overlooked. It had already been examined for fingerprints and carried none. There were a few plastic bags containing soil and debris stacked on the footway that they had to climb over.

'It can't be all of what they dug out,' Benoist said. 'There must be more somewhere.'

It didn't take them long to find where. More plastic bags were stacked in another recess and a few had fallen into the water which had risen around them. There was no sign of any tools.

'They planned this one well,' Darcy commented. 'They got rid of everything before they entered the bank. I reckon they were ready to go the night before and tidied up behind them so they could make a quick getaway.'

Pel's face was grim as he crawled along the tunnel. Although it was a hurriedly constructed affair, nothing had been left to chance. The boards that held the sides and roof in place had all been carefully cut to size.

At the end of the tunnel, bricks had been removed from a wall and stacked carefully to one side. Beyond the hole was the bank's stationery store and the back of a wooden cupboard. A large portion of it had been cut away and about them in the tunnel were crumpled sheets, forms and notepaper bearing the bank's heading.

Scrambling into the store among the trampled paper and files, Pel looked about him. The cupboard had a lock and key.

'They locked it after them,' Lotier said. 'As they left. And dragged it into place from the back. That's why all the stuff's stacked in the corridor. When they arrived they cut a hole in the back so they could push stuff out. As soon as they'd got enough out of the way, they managed to move the cupboard and one of them climbed through. It would be quite a job. In a small space like that. He hauled out the rest of the stuff and dragged the cupboard further from the wall so that the rest of them could climb in. After that, all they had to do was wait for the staff to arrive.'

Pel was thoughtful. 'But how did they know where to cut the hole in the cupboard?' he asked. 'They could have spent half the night trying to cut holes and finding the saw up against boxes, files, bound blocks of paper. Find out who was responsible for the stationery, Daniel. They might know how it was stacked. Come to that,' he ended, 'how did they know the cupboard was made of wood?'

Pel's conference was also attended by the Chief who was in a foul temper because he felt thoroughly humiliated. He had always felt he ran a good department that produced results and the robbery at the Crédit Rural had shaken him to the core. Turgot was wondering if suicide might fit the bill.

They had struggled to avoid bloodshed and in their concern for the safety of the hostages had allowed themselves to be led up the garden path. The robbers had never had any intention of shooting, or even holding, the hostages. The point of the whole charade had been to concentrate the police round the bank and the area of the Church of St Philibert, so as to leave the streets round the Place Nozay clear for a swift getaway.

They knew that now but it was always easy to be wise after the event. Chivvied by the Search and Assist people and the sharpshooters from Lyons, to say nothing of the enormous numbers of policemen involved in surrounding the Rue de la Queste area, setting up listening gear, preparing to abseil down the front of the building from the roof, and pondering all the other possibilities that had been considered, Turgot had had quite a lot on his plate.

'It was a put-up job,' he explained bitterly. 'That telephone call that raised the alarm – they deliberately took their eyes off the hostages for a minute or two before they were gagged so that it got through.'

Sitting at the back of the room, Nosjean decided that quite a lot of people had been taking their eyes off things lately – Distaing, for instance, and the staff of the Musée des Arts Modernes.

'It gives us all red faces,' the Chief growled. 'It must be one of the most daring robberies ever.'

There had been other daring raids on banks. Robbers had tunnelled through sewers before, or entered through ceilings from flats situated above. But these had occurred in Marseilles or Nice where one expected that sort of thing to happen, not in this city which was their pride and joy.

'There'll be a full enquiry,' the Chief said. But, he admitted on the quiet, he didn't regard the case as having been mishandled. 'Turgot did everything he was supposed to do,' he decided.

Except make guesses, Pel thought.

Benoist, the inspector of sewers, who was sitting in to give advice, outlined the sewerage plan. 'There are different systems,' he pointed out. 'And they're all designed for minimum maintenance so there's no regular inspection. The first is a combined one in which one set of sewers receives both foul sewage and the rainfall run-off from roofs, roads and surfaces. The second has two patterns, one of which takes the effluent to the sewage works for treatment, and another which delivers comparatively clean surface water to the nearest point of outfall. There's also a third by which surface drainage from houses is discharged into the effluent sewers. The sewer they used is what might be called a clean water sewer and it has ventilation to remove poisonous, explosive or corrosive gases produced by decomposition and other causes.'

Pel lit a cigarette. Fat chance he had of giving them up, he thought. Avoid stress, the adverts said. He lived and breathed stress.

'Near the Crédit Rural,' Benoist added, 'there are two smaller sewers – both large enough for a man to move easily along them – designed to remove water from the streets during heavy rainstorms. In one of these there's an unlit recess from which the tunnel was driven.'

'We ought to have realized what they were up to,' Turgot said bitterly. 'There's a ventilation column in the street almost outside the bank.'

'The route they took', Pel continued the story, 'was under the Rue Doctor Chaussiet, the Rue de la Poste and the Rue du Château, emerging in the Place Nozay. It was marked with a line on the diagram we found and looked like the tail of a kite and was carefully worked out to bring them up outside the perimeter we put up. One among them was either a cop with experience of traffic or they'd watched the traffic and worked it out – or both. The Place Nozay brought them on to a direct route out of the city.

'They were waiting when the bank staff arrived,' he went on. 'They took the customers hostage to make it look better, and they knew perfectly well when the under-manager arrived because someone had told them, as someone had told them the day when the surplus old notes were waiting to be removed. The shots were intended to draw every policeman in the city to the bank. When they were there, they got away by the route they had arrived. They were well clear before Labarre managed to struggle to the window. Were the roads out of the city guarded?'

'No,' Turgot admitted. 'Because the gang were all in the bank. We'd circled the whole area. Every street and every building. They couldn't get out.'

'But they did, didn't they?' Pel said quietly.

Gilbaud, the manager of Crédit Rural, a small pink man who looked as though he always dined well, explained how the bank worked. 'Every branch has a certain sum in cash in hand,' he said. 'If at the end of the day or week it has more than it needs it sends the surplus in shoddy notes to central headquarters. Ours was already packed and waiting to go in special sacks.'

'Same time every week?' Pel asked.

'No. I vary the days and time.'

'So someone would have to know?'

'Only me. I telephone from my office.'

'Would anyone else know?'

'No.'

'What about the staff?'

'They've been with us for ages. Apart from the youngest clerk. They're entirely trustworthy. The bank makes sure of it. So do I.'

A huge plan of the bank had been pinned to a blackboard, together with a plan of the sewers.

'We start', Pel said, indicating it, 'by examining how the tunnel was made. They had a distance of around thirty metres to cover from the sewer to the back of the storage cupboard. It's not a lot to experts and I expect they'd all read those books that were written after the war about people trying to escape from German prison camps. If my memory serves me right, they all gave everything in great detail.

'The tunnel was around eighty centimetres by fifty. Not a lot of soil to remove, especially as it's soft and sandy. Half-way along they built in a small recess twice the width of the tunnel where a man could crouch. It was to enable them to pass each other, something that was otherwise impossible. They used it also to store the final bags of soil they'd removed from the digging. To shore the walls up they used pieces of plank – '

'Of cheap whitewood or plywood,' Leguyader pointed out. 'Eighty centimetres tall, fifty wide. The roof was held up by longer ones, sixty wide, resting on the uprights.'

'And they took no chances,' Pel said. 'They were set against the wall only a few centimetres apart. They must have used over sixty sets of them and they'd been cut by a circular saw. We need to know *which* saw. They got in at night. It would be a good time because nobody's about at night these days. They're all watching *Dallas*. They needed light but they didn't tap the electricity, so they must have used heavy battery lamps. There must have been at least six. One each. Find out where they came from. They also used a military field telephone. Where did that come from? Plastic fertilizer bags were used to haul the waste away. They probably intended them originally to haul away the loot but the bank obligingly placed the notes in canvas bags which were suitably sized for handling in the tunnel. Where did the fertilizer bags come from? When we know these things we might make some headway.'

He turned brusquely to Benoist. 'I shall want a list of all your employees,' he said. 'Every man who works in the sewers or who has worked in them during the last five years. I'll also want the names of all employees who had access to plans of the sewers. Anybody who could have known that it was possible to climb through that man-hole in the Place Nozay and end up under the Crédit Rural.'

Pel bluntly made it clear to his team that everybody would be on duty twenty-four hours a day. 'You'll be missing meals and sleep,' he pointed out grimly. 'You also won't be seeing your homes much till this thing's sorted out. Almost seventy million francs were stolen and we don't rest till we get it back. Furthermore, I might remind you that this is also a murder enquiry. Somebody killed Robert Meluc. He was part of the gang but we still want to know who killed him and exactly why.'

As Pel looked over them, he wondered how their wives and girl-friends would take the overtime – if twenty-four hours a day could be considered overtime. Whenever anything big occurred, the tensions at home always rose, and it was God help those women who weren't occupied and didn't know how to be happy in their own company. What did they all do when their men didn't appear for days on end and when they did were exhausted, complaining about their feet, frustrated from trying to find something that wouldn't appear, snappy because of failure, and not concerned with the fiendish expectations of the marriage vows? It was then that the women forgot the bit about being faithful 'till death do us part'.

7

Meanwhile, Nosjean was still hot on the trail of Colette Esterhazy. He discovered that she was well known at the University, more, it seemed, for her looks than for her chances of getting a degree, which were nevertheless excellent. It seemed that not only the students but the tutors, too, had been quick to notice her beauty.

'She was quite clever,' one of them admitted. 'I told her she was wasting her time worrying about a degree. I told her she should get hold of a studio and start painting. I said it might take time but she was bound to make it in the end. She did as I said but she kept on with her studies all the same. She had skill . . .' He paused. '. . . if not a lot of artistic imagination.'

Nosjean guessed that one of them at least had slept with the girl but, judging by their descriptions of her, it seemed to have been inevitable. From the University, he found his way to the studio of a man called Albert Courtrand, who had painted her. He was a huge, amiable man with a beard and an untidy thatch of hair that was spotted with paint. His studio was full of paintings of nudes, all a little too gorgeous to be true. 'Sure,' he told Nosjean. 'I knew her. She often modelled for me. That's her.'

He showed him a portrait of a nude girl sitting on a stool tying a bandanna round her hair; the light fell across the subject, highlighting the curves of flesh. She was outstandingly beautiful.

'It isn't exaggerated either,' Courtrand said. 'She was one of the most beautiful girls I've ever met.' He gestured at the other paintings. 'Those are models which I've titivated up a bit. Improvements on the nose. The eyes. The bust. The legs. The lips. So they'll sell better. I make my living from nudes so I always make them as gorgeous as I can. But not old Esterhazy. You didn't have to improve on her in any way. There was nothing you *could* improve. She was perfect.'

'In every way?'

'In every way,' Courtrand said stoutly. 'She was good-tempered and happy. Tell her to take off and she took off without wondering if it were cold.'

'Take off?' Nosjean had visions of a naked girl flying round the studio with her arms outspread.

'Clothes. Take off. Put on. Clothes.'

'Ah.' Light dawned. 'Did you ever see her apart from her being a model?'

Courtrand was wary. 'We sometimes ate a meal together,' he said. 'Had a drink together.' He grinned. 'Went to bed together.'

'Was she your mistress?'

'No, man. But I enjoyed sex and so did she. But I have a wife so we kept it quiet. I hope all this isn't going to find its way into the papers.'

'No reason why it should,' Nosjean said. 'I'm grateful for your frankness.' He left Courtrand with a lightness in his step, not sure that he was really getting anywhere but hopeful that he might.

When Nosjean at last managed to find him, Leygues seemed shattered. He had just flown home and still looked exhausted. A tall, good-looking man in his fifties, he had a high forehead and a fine straight nose and chiselled chin. Judging by what Nosjean had heard of her, he'd have made a good match for Colette Esterhazy.

'She made her first application to the museum last year,' he said. 'In the usual way. We agreed to let her copy. It was a Picasso. She completed that and then decided to tackle something harder – a Clouet. She did it very well, too. Then she asked about the Rousseau and the Paot. Since she'd been so enthusiastic, I gave permission that she should be allowed.'

'Even to taking the pictures from their frames?'

Leygues flushed. 'Yes. Even that. She claimed she could do the work better that way, that she could get nearer. She studied the things with a magnifying glass to get the brush strokes right. I gave permission.'

'Have you ever done this before? Removed the pictures from their frames?'

'No.'

'Why for her?'

Leygues drew a deep breath. 'You never saw her,' he said. 'You had to see her to understand.'

'Did you ever see her outside the museum?'

'What has that to do with it?'

'It might explain why you gave permission.'

Leygues drew in his breath again. 'I am the director of a museum and art gallery,' he said stiffly. 'I don't chase young girls who come to learn about art.'

Nosjean didn't believe him.

From the portrait that he'd built up of Colette Esterhazy, it began to seem to Nosjean that Leygues' decision to allow her to have pictures out of their frames was not all that unusual. There appeared to be a lot of people about who would happily have lain down and allowed Colette Esterhazy to walk up their backs in spiked heels. She had everything in her favour, but she had never, it seerned, taken advantage of it – save for apparently seducing Arthur Leygues and Marc Distaing into allowing her to walk away with two pictures worth a fortune.

It only left her parents. The University supplied their address. She came from Beauvais and it meant a long journey. Nosjean did it on the Sunday and took Mijo Lehmann with him for the day out.

Colette Esterhazy's parents lived in a large house on the outskirts of the town. Her father was a lawyer and they lived in comfortable circumstances. He was a very good-looking man and it was obvious that his wife had once been beautiful. They were gentle and welcoming and seemed devoted to each other so that it was clear Colette Esterhazy had inherited from them not only her good looks but also her happy nature.

They were clearly horrified by what had happened. 'She was always such a good girl,' her mother said. 'And so clever. She was good at her studies at school, and when she discovered she was good at art she made the switch to it easily. We thought she had a great future before her.'

'We were worried, though,' her father pointed out. 'You read so much about artists, don't you?' He cleared his throat while his wife raised her eyebrows.

You did indeed, Nosjean thought. 'What about men?' he asked. 'I get the impression that she's very beautiful. It would seem normal that men would chase her.'

'Oh, they do,' Madame Esterhazy said. 'But it doesn't seem to worry her. She's always modest about herself. I don't think she realizes how beautiful she is. That's why she's always so nice, so kind. There isn't an atom of selfishness in her.'

Nosjean seemed to be investigating a paragon of virtue.

'Did any of them come here?' he asked.

'Oh, of course. There was Yvon Tisch. And George de Vannes. They were both very wealthy and we rather hoped . . .' Madame Esterhazy shrugged. 'But she seems set on a career in art and nothing came of either of them.'

'Anybody who wasn't local?'

'One or two. But nobody more than once or twice. She doesn't seem to be all that interested.'

She must have been interested in someone, Nosjean decided. He couldn't imagine a girl as beautiful, gifted, kind and naïve as this one was supposed to be thinking up a clever scheme to steal two valuable paintings without help. In which case, there must have been some man in the background, playing Svengali to her Trilby.

'When did you last see her?'

'Some time ago now. She lives her own life. She's old enough. And she has a high moral standard.'

Not all that high, if what he'd heard was true, Nosjean thought. But perhaps it was high enough for the day and age. He was no one to talk himself. He had been living with Mijo Lehmann for some time now and his sisters – three of them, all older, all spinsters, all less attractive and less sophisticated – were still dropping strong hints that it was time they married and started producing a family.

'You see,' Madame Esterhazy said, 'she wants to get on with her life. I sometimes ask if she doesn't feel like settling down and marrying and she always says, "Not yet." She feels marriage would stop her career dead. She thinks she can do well as an artist. In fact she's been told so by one of her tutors at the University. He advised her to forget her degree and just get on with painting. But, having started on it, she feels that a degree would still be a good idea. It would be there, she says, in case anything happened, so that if for some reason she couldn't paint she could always turn to reviewing, teaching or working for an art gallery. She's a very sensible girl.'

But also a girl who could easily be led, Nosjean decided. Perhaps she had felt she was doing someone a favour, being kind, helping a lame dog over a stile, doing good works. There *were* people like that. Perhaps she had thought it was of benefit to the less fortunate in the world to lift the two paintings. Perhaps she was going to give the proceeds to charity. There had been dafter things, he considered. But not many.

8

Unlike Nosjean the bank investigators were getting nowhere fast. An estimated sixty-seven million francs in
old notes and jewels had disappeared from the Banque
Crédit Rural and they hadn't even started to produce any
evidence.

They had no names. Not one.

To find out what the gang looked like, Pel tried mug
shots of possible suspects on the staff and the customers
who had been at the bank during the hold-up.

'We couldn't see,' one of them said. 'We were lying on
our faces and they wore stocking masks.'

'Could you see nothing at all?' Darcy asked. 'The
smallest thing would help.'

'One had long fair hair,' one of the girl clerks offered
helpfully. 'It looked as if he washed it regularly. It was
very fluffy and shiny.'

After scrambling about in a tunnel from a sewer?
Darcy found it hard to believe.

But it was about all they got. There were references to
marks that looked like scars, a pointed nose – but no one
was sure because features were flattened by the nylon
stockings the gang had worn over their faces. One
seemed to be fair but under the nylon stocking he could
well have been off-brown.

Only old Bridier had seen them without their stocking
masks and he wasn't very helpful.

'Were they wearing some other sort of masks when they came out of the manhole?' Pel asked. They had to be, he decided. For occasions like this villains usually wore Mickey Mouse or Donald Duck faces or something of that sort. On the other hand you couldn't climb out of a manhole wearing a protective hat and a Mickey Mouse mask without raising some sort of question. People didn't usually hold parties down a sewer. But he also knew the general public were so unobservant that they might ignore anything, or if they didn't ignore it, they wouldn't report it.

Old Bridier was vague and offhand and persisted in addressing half his remarks to the dog. 'We knew a Pel once,' he said. 'Didn't we, Tou-Tou? He was a policeman, too. He used to direct traffic on the corner where we lived.'

Pel frowned. He didn't like being equated with other policemen. He felt he was unique and he certainly didn't direct traffic. He tried to push his questions but the old man was less than exact.

'Normal height,' he said cheerfully, enjoying the first excitement and interest he'd had for years. 'Same as everybody else. Weren't they, Tou-Tou? Or were they a bit taller?'

The dog showed no interest either way.

'Did you get a good look at them?' Pel asked.

'Oh, excellent,' Bridier said. 'I can describe them if you wish.'

'I do wish,' Pel said sharply. What in God's name, he thought, did the old fool think he was asking questions for?

'Well . . .' Bridier paused to think. 'One had a wide mouth, with deep lines on either side of his nose. As if he sneered a lot. That sort. That's right, isn't it, Tou-Tou? You saw him also. I remember that very clearly. One had . . . well . . . sort of slanting eyes. A bit like a Chinese. But he wasn't a Chinese, was he, Tou-Tou? If you under-stand what I mean. They had very definite faces.'

'Definite? In what way?'

'Just definite. Tou-Tou would tell you.'

'I'd rather you did,' Pel said coldly.

'Well,' Bridier said huffily, 'the third man who came out had a very red face. As if he drank a lot. Reddish complexion. That sort of thing. One had a dark skin. Arab. Something like that.'

This was a new one. None of the hostages had men-tioned a man with a dark skin.

'Go on,' Pel said. 'Do you remember any more?'

'One had hollow eyes. Very hollow. As if his eyes were sunk in his head. But, of course – ' Bridier laughed – 'it might have been the shadow caused by the peak of his hat. One of them had a thin nose and wrinkles round his eyes. Very marked wrinkles. As if he laughed a lot. Or screwed up his eyes against the sun. I know about wrin-kles. I've got them. They're from spending a lot of time in Algeria when I was young. I used to help build dams. Everybody in Algeria had lines on their faces. Even the women. In fact – ' He saw Pel's frown and hurried on. 'Oh, yes, and one of them had a moustache.'

There seemed a possible lead. They had the identity kit man with them and he worked out six pictures. They were none of them very satisfactory because old Bridier, though he could remember the particular features he had mentioned, couldn't remember anything else. Perhaps the dog could, Pel thought bitterly. He'd have to ask Leguyader if there were any way of finding out.

He looked angrily at what they'd produced. A man with a wide mouth and deep lines running down on either side of his nose. As if he sneered a lot. One with a red face. One like an Arab. One with hollow or deeply set eyes. One with a thin nose. One moustache. They all seemed to have at least one very clear and distinct feature that ought easily to be noticed. Almost too easily noticed. Pel wondered, in fact, if old Bridier had made them up. Witnesses such as Bridier often did for the kudos and excitement it gave them. When they'd checked back with the hostages none of them could remember a man with dark skin. Perhaps old Bridier had been tired and bored. He had soon wearied under the questioning, so perhaps he'd offered the descriptions to stop them badgering him.

Most people, Pel thought, when you asked for a description, went blank. Old Bridier had gone blank. The people in the bank had gone blank. They seemed to have been there most of the day with their eyes shut. They remembered that the gang had all worn overalls, stocking masks and rubber gloves of the type housewives used for washing up, in gaudy pink, yellow or blue, but there wasn't anything else they remembered: no twisted fingers, no limps, no down-at-heel shoes, no coloured socks. Out of the lot of them, only one had noticed that one of the gang had fair hair and he'd worn it long and appeared to wash it regularly. And even that was surely doubtful. It was the same old story. You could have stood the young Brigitte Bardot in front of the average citizen and asked for a description and got an answer something like, 'Well, she's got a face. With real eyes.' To most people, other people's faces were as blank as puddings.

As they returned to headquarters they passed the Hôtel Central and decided in their frustration that they needed a drink in its hallowed precincts instead of in the crowded and smoky Bar Transvaal which was the bar the police used behind headquarters.

The Hôtel Central was the most prestigious hotel in the city, as was obvious from the number of American tourists who used it, and the Hôtel Central tried to make them feel at home. It had a Texas Bar, where they served drinks so cold they made your teeth ache, a New York Grill and a Manhattan Cocktail Lounge. The dining-room was known throughout the city as Le Hamburger from its habit of including even that delicacy among its courses. The French were all for making the Americans feel at home but they sometimes felt that in this case the management let their enthusiasm run away with them – especially in winter when there were few tourists about and the people who ate and drank there were mostly French.

Pel and Darcy were met by the manager, a tall, well-fleshed individual who gave them a gracious smile. Despite the smile, he didn't really like seeing the police. They had helped him more than once but it made no difference. Police about the place could give it a bad name.

Because of the cold, Pel ordered a whisky. He even asked Darcy if he'd like one, too, and was shaken when he said he would. Darcy didn't normally drink spirits during the day and he'd expected him to say no.

They began to discuss the case which was becoming increasingly bizarre and extremely frustrating for, although every corner of the bank had been dusted down, there was no sign of any fingerprints.

'They didn't have to crack the safe. They had the keys. They got them from Gilbaud,' said Darcy sourly.

Gradually it was becoming clearer what had happened. 'It looks as if this bunch were very thorough – providing for any contingency,' said Pel. The gang had guessed just where the police would place their guarded perimeter round the bank and had made sure that their escape would emerge behind the police backs.

'Could we have an informer in the Hôtel de Police?' Darcy asked desperately. They looked at each other, both immediately thinking of Misset. But, they decided, even Misset wouldn't do that. They'd suspected him more than once of passing on snippets of information to the press. But they couldn't imagine even he would pass on information as important as this to a gang of criminals, a gang moreover who had surely been responsible for Robert Meluc's death, and the death of the old man in the bank who had died of a heart attack after being coshed. Besides, for once Misset had shown intelligence over the street guide, and had acted promptly if not quite in time. Regrettably Pel knew they didn't have a suspect.

'The type who worked it out wasn't necessarily a serving cop,' Pel suggested hopefully. 'A retired cop? A cop who was kicked out? A cop who was bent and was retired a little early? Do we know anyone like that? A man like that would be able to work out from a Blay guide the sort of deviation that we'd fix up round the Crédit Rural – especially if he'd worked in Traffic and especially if he knew the city. I could work out roughly which roads Pomereu would seal off and which ones he'd use to keep the traffic moving. So could you. Some cop who'd had experience – even some years ago.'

'It's an idea, Patron. It's worth going into.'

Pel spread the diagram Minet had found in Meluc's wallet alongside Pomereu's plan and placed their glasses on the corners. For the most part it matched.

'Just a few places where they guessed wrong,' he pointed out. 'This little bit here. And this one – the Rue de Soissons. And they've gone a bit wrong round the Rue Danton. But in the main they've got it right and the mistakes made no difference. Rue de l'Arquebuse. Boulevard de Sévigné. Rue de la Liberté. Rue Bossuet. Rue Monge. It wasn't a bad guess.'

'What are these crosses?' Darcy asked. 'Four round the perimeter. And two at the end of the tail.'

'Six crosses altogether,' Pel pointed out. 'Six in the gang. The two at the end of the tail are obviously where they emerged at the Place Nozay. Bars where they watched the manhole for a while? The others? Routes they marked off for the getaway. The one at the end of the Rue Bossuet indicates access to the Rue du Drapeau and the north. The one on Sévigné the route to the RN5 and the west, the other two routes south to the RN74 and the RN996. They've got it all worked out.'

'But which did they take?'

'Perhaps they'd been watching those spots to see which was best. Let's check. Get the troops out asking questions. Let's find out if anybody we know or would like to know lives round there. And let's have Lage go through all our files to see if he can find an ex-cop with a record. Because if he can, he's probably our man and will lead us to the other five.'

'Or twenty-five,' Darcy pointed out drily. 'We don't know how big this gang is. These six might only be the active members. I wonder if any of them ever worked with Albert Spaggiarsi.'

Albert Spaggiarsi was an anarchist who in 1976 had masterminded a spectacular sixty-million-franc robbery of the Société Générale bank in Nice, also by tunnelling through a sewer.

'It's possible,' Pel admitted. 'Let's ask. I reckon it took Spaggiarsi's lot a bit longer, though. They did it over the weekend and even tapped the electricity and cooked a meal in the vault while they were emptying it. But Spaggiarsi did it the hard way. They had to get into the vault because they didn't have the keys. Ours went in through the stationery store, which doesn't have reinforced walls. Nothing on that floor does. Only the vault's reinforced, and they got into that because they'd got the keys by threatening to do for Gilbaud's family. And while we were making threatening noises at the front on the surface they got out at the back below ground and disappeared in Meluc's van.'

When they reached the Hôtel de Police they called on

Leguyader at the Forensic Lab. He had dabbled his fingers in some powder they had found scattered round the washroom at the bank and sniffed them, his nose wrinkling like a dog at a rabbit hole. He had at least one answer they wanted. He wasn't everybody's favourite but they had to admit his findings often contributed to the success of a case because, if nothing else, he knew his job.

'Talcum powder,' he announced. 'That's what it is. I got some of my wife's and compared it. Made from magnesium silicate. Often tinted faintly pink. This was. It's a cheap brand, I'd say. It can be bought at any perfumery or the Nouvelles Galeries.'

'Any indication of why it's there?'

Leguyader smiled triumphantly. 'None at all,' he said.

Back to square one. They'd established that the powder they'd found was the same stuff mothers sprinkled on their babies' bottoms after a bath but not why a gang of bank robbers had tossed it about during a bank raid.

It was quite obvious by this time that the police had been well and truly fooled. They had been led to believe they were facing a dangerous situation where there might well be murders, even that they might be facing terrorists who were robbing the bank to raise funds for one of their assassination attempts. But no assassinations were expected – not even of tax inspectors who were the only people apart from top politicians whom anyone would want to bump off without good reason – and in fact, they'd been facing nothing but a good old-fashioned robbery, planned with considerable cunning.

They enquired at the houses in the Place Nozay surrounding the manhole by which the gang had entered and left the bank.

'They must have carried equipment,' Pel pointed out.

'Picks. Shovels. Crowbars. Hammers. Saws. Plastic bags to remove the dirt they were digging out. Somebody must have seen something.'

But nobody had. It was too much, he thought savagely, to expect an intelligent human being to notice anything out of the ordinary.

One or two people mentioned seeing workmen but they hadn't seen them enter the manhole, couldn't describe them, didn't know which day they saw them, and weren't even sure what job they were engaged on. The police checked them out as far as they could. One or two had even seen a grey car hanging around in the square some time before and had now begun to wonder, as they put two and two together, if it had had anything to do with the robbery.

'It more than likely had,' Pel said. 'Did you get the number?'

'It was too far away.'

'What make was it?'

'It was broadside-on and I couldn't see the bonnet.'

Pel's face had begun to take on the look of a small boy who had expected a bicycle for his birthday and received a ballpoint pen.

It began to seem that the gang had made a detailed survey of the Place Nozay, doubtless counting the number of people who used it, and coming up with the answer, 'Not many,' had decided it was safe to masquerade as sewerage workers and open the manhole from time to time.

This theory was given added force when they learned that at the Bar du Nord on the corner of Rémy and Foch a man had made a habit of sitting for long hours in the window with a drink, watching the road west.

'He had a notebook and pencil in his hand,' the barman said.

'What was he like?' Pel asked.

The barman rubbed his nose. 'He wore a black wind-cheater,' he said.

'Lots of people wear black windcheaters. But some people have two or three.' Pel was growing frustrated to the point of sarcasm. 'Of different colours. And they sometimes even swap them about. What was he like? The man himself.'

'His hair was short. As if he kept it well trimmed.'

'Tall?'

'Medium.'

'Thickset?'

'Fairly. But not too much.'

'In other words, he was medium.'

'Yes.'

'What about his face?'

'We never saw it. He was always staring out of the window, with his back to us.'

'Did *no one* see him? Other customers?'

'He came usually in the late afternoon. There aren't many around at that time. It's quiet. They mostly start coming in when the offices close. A quick drink to stiffen them for meeting the wife and kids. Or else early in the morning when we were rushed off our feet serving breakfast coffee and rolls.'

'Didn't you see his features at all?'

'Not really.'

'Complexion? Sallow? Fair?'

'Medium.'

There were other bars at which they thought they might have more luck, but if somebody had sat watching the roads at the junctions of Liberté and Bossuet or Arquebuse and Monge they had managed to make themselves inconspicuous because they hadn't been noticed.

'So which way did they go?' Pel snarled. 'We seem to have a choice between north, east, west and south.'

By this time Crédit Rural was functioning again. The front office was still full of people clamouring to know what had happened to their safe deposit boxes and the counter staff were hard at it. On the surface, except for a couple of policemen on the door, it looked normal enough. Behind the scenes, however, Fingerprints were still hard at work, covering the whole premises and checking the dabs they had found with Records. They'd found lots of them but they all belonged to the bank staff, with a few additional ones from customers. The gang had worn their rubber gloves at all times, so fingerprints weren't really expected.

In the offices behind and in the narrow corridors, large policemen brushed shoulders – and not only shoulders – with buxom typists heading for the canteen or the ladies' room. It was a confrontation that pleased both sides and Misset, at least, managed to get a date out of it. All the paper, envelopes, forms and files from the stationery store had been stacked in the office of Annette Didon, the manager's secretary, adding more than a little to her discomfort and confusion, and the Fingerprints boys were busy inside the wooden cupboard.

One of them was holding a circle of wood. 'Cut out with a keyhole saw,' he said.

'Why a *wooden* cupboard?' Pel asked Gilbaud. 'I thought bank furniture was steel.'

Gilbaud looked both sheepish and defensive. 'This is an old branch – the oldest in the city. We still have some of the original furniture which is considered antique. It's heavy and it was decided at head office to use it, but it's due to go.' He spoke fast.

'But it hadn't gone,' Pel said bitterly. 'Had it? And the gang cut a hole in it to remove the contents and shift the cupboard so they could climb through.'

They had nothing to work on but one smudged foot-print on one of the sheets of scattered notepaper in the stationery store-room but they eventually found the car-pentry firm who had cut the boards. The man who had ordered and collected them was described as short and squarely built. He had seemed nervous and had asked for a bill. The name he had signed with was Jacques Dupont but there were hundreds of Jacques Duponts. It was the name men signed in hotel registers when they were having a dirty weekend.

'It sounds like Meluc,' Darcy said, fishing in his brief-case for the photograph Aimedieu had obtained for him.

It *was* Meluc. The clerk in the office identified him without doubt.

'He thought I didn't know him,' he said. 'But I used to work for Bricolage Secours and he used to come there regularly for cement and tiles and things. He said he'd been told to provide them but didn't intend to slave with a hand saw. He asked for them to be made from old off-cuts and bits of left-over plywood. I'd know him anywhere. He was always a bit of a shyster who used poor materials and charged top prices.'

Pel was more cheerful as they left. It was the first mistake the gang had made. If Meluc hadn't been lazy they wouldn't have found even this frail lead.

'But he *was* involved,' he mused.

The telephone and the battery lamps had been hired from an electrical firm in the Arsenal district also by Meluc. They had not been returned and the owner was far from pleased to learn that, when they *were* found, they would be retained as police exhibits for the court to see when the trial finally took place – *if* it took place.

'That stuff means money to me,' he snorted.

'It means prison for someone,' Darcy pointed out drily.

By this time the newspapers were becoming abrasive

about the affair, doing their usual act of being wise after the event and jeering at the police. They never mentioned their own boobs, of course. Newspapers liked to imply that, like God, they were models of infallibility. Unpopularity didn't worry the police too much, though. One half of the nation had always regarded them as the tools of a fascist dictatorship, the other half as half-baked, wet-behind-the-ears dolts who couldn't arrest a small boy on a bike. Some considered they were given to breaking heads for pleasure, others that they existed merely to be targets for brickbats and pieces of paving stone flung by students. At the very least, motorists considered them interfering busybodies, while old ladies who found them standing on corners wanted to know why they weren't stamping out crime.

The pressure wasn't allowed to die down. There had been plenty of telephone calls from people who saw a little easy money in the reward and thought they might pick it up. One woman had seen a man covered with blood at St Seine. But nobody else had, certainly not old Bridier, who had watched them emerge from the manhole. Every known crook and con man was checked again. Hotel registers – especially those of back-street establishments – were checked in case their men had holed up.

There were also the usual hoaxers who thought it funny to burden the already overburdened police with false alarms. One or two were picked up and were now contemplating their misdemeanours in 72, Rue d'Auxonne. A woman clairvoyant said the money no longer existed. It had been flashed, she claimed, to Mars by a streak of lightning. Every postbag brought letters, most of the anonymous ones accusing the owners of noisy dogs or people who refused to turn down their televisions, had sons with motorbikes or even simply, in one case, hung out washing on the Sabbath.

They did a round-up of everybody in the city with a known habit of removing things that didn't belong to them. Every cop in the Hôtel de Police was on the streets and a few were even brought in from the surrounding districts to help. For a while life became very rugged for the city's criminal fraternity.

'Holy Mother of God,' one of them said indignantly as he was hauled in. 'You can't lift a roll of insulating tape these days without being accused of pinching sixty million francs.'

There were a few false alarms. A man reported to have been flashing a large number of high-denomination notes in a bar at Talant turned out to have just cashed in his insurance at the age of sixty-five. A woman who boasted to a neighbour that her husband had come into money was interviewed when the neighbour reported it to the police and the husband was picked up at Métaux de Bourgogne where he worked. It turned out that he had just sold a car. But the car's distance indicator had been tampered with and he had his name taken and the man who had bought the car indignantly demanded his money back. The following evening, one of the city cops was called to a back-street fight between two women. The wife of the man who had fiddled the car had just blacked the eye of the neighbour who had informed on her husband.

Finally, another man getting on a train for the north with a large sealed canvas sack was spotted by someone buying a ticket for Lyons to go and see his sister. A telephone message resulted in the suspect being hauled off the train at Montbard. He turned out to be an engineer on his way to Paris with an urgent spare part for the printing press of a Paris newspaper. When he was finally allowed to go on his way it was too late and when he arrived in Paris the paper had lost thousands of copies. As a result the paper was now indignantly threatening to sue the police, the railway and the man who'd made the report.

9

The next day, Pel had to attend the funeral of Judge Polverari. Everybody who had known the old man was there – from the Chief downwards, and including Judge Casteou who had already been appointed to take his place. The funeral was a suitably sombre affair, with the black and silver drapings and the long cadences of the priest's voice. The weather had suddenly become bitterly cold and they stood in a circle round the grave while the clouds built up like sheets of lead over the hills to the north.

That evening the snow came. The temperature had dropped until it became that particularly cheerless cold that always precedes a blizzard and the snow started in the afternoon, falling in a blinding white whirling cloud that made it difficult for Pel to reach home. Even as he arrived, the sanding and gritting lorries were out and he noticed a snow plough in the village ready for the morning. Evidently someone had read the forecasts.

'You'll need something warm on tomorrow,' his wife commented. 'Put on that thick sweater I knitted for you.'

'Of course, Geneviève *de mon coeur*,' Pel said, smiling.

But it was a false smile. Madame Pel believed her household duties included knitting for her husband but, despite her ability with money, she was no knitter and what she created, though warm enough, could hardly be called becoming. Pel decided to take the sweater with him and leave it at the back of the cupboard in his office.

Muffled to the eyebrows and wearing so many clothes he could hardly move his arms, he set off for the city next morning with some trepidation. But the snow plough had been ahead of him and it wasn't as difficult as he'd expected. At the junction with the main road a lorry with a trailer had jack-knifed and gone into the ditch. Its driver was standing near it looking shocked and dazed, talking to two policemen from a patrol car as they waited for a crane. Traffic accidents were none of Pel's business and he pressed on, thankful he hadn't been around when it happened.

At the Hôtel de Police, it took him some time to thaw out. He'd had the car heater going full blast because he was as warm-blooded as a frog and liked to live par-boiled, and the walk from the car-park left him chilled to the marrow. He stood in his office as though petrified until Annie Saxe arrived with the newspapers and a bundle of letters for him.

'I've been through the papers,' she said enthusiastically. 'I've marked a few things I thought you might be interested in. It'll save you having to go through the whole lot.'

It would also, Pel thought with a glare, take the edge off opening a brand new paper.

The newspapers were actually just an excuse for Annie to get out of the sergeants' room. Misset had decided she was a pushover. Despite her aggressive manner, he considered that she wasn't big enough to put up much resistance. Misset had enormous confidence in his woman-killer tactics and didn't expect problems. His approach was well tested and proved, and he knew she was unmarried because he'd looked at her file. Misset preferred them unmarried because it was always possible that a woman you picked might turn out to have a weight-lifter for a husband.

He had opened his campaign with a comment on her car. 'Very sexy,' he said.

It had made her wary immediately. Her car was a Citroën 2CV, one of the old Deux Chevaux which were noted for the fact that they wouldn't start, were uncomfortable to ride in, had the same suspension as a jelly and got blown off the road trying to overtake lorries. Annie's had been used for years by her father in the woods round Belfort before he'd given it to her and when in motion it usually smelled strongly of burning. Misset's comment had been stupid.

She pushed him briskly to the back of her mind and concentrated on Pel, wise enough to know that he was the one who mattered.

'You look cold, sir,' she said cheerfully.

'I *am* cold,' Pel snapped.

She helped by energetically yanking away several layers of clothing, almost tearing his arm off in the process. 'You need something warm,' she announced. 'How about coffee?'

'Send Didier Darras across to the Bar Transvaal for a bottle of rum.'

The coffee turned up within five minutes and the rum a minute later. Annie Saxe sloshed it into Pel's mug with joyous abandon and he began to see that enthusiasm in the young might have its advantages.

The papers were still obsessed with the hold-up at Crédit Rural. The headlines varied from BANK DEATH WATCH PUZZLE: 23 HOSTAGES FACED GUNS to HOLD-UP ARREST FOILED: POLICE STILL BAFFLED BY ESCAPE. The headlines were no worse than normal, Pel decided, tossing them aside. Just the usual police knocking campaign.

He was just beginning to feel better when Darcy appeared. 'Who made the coffee?' he asked.

'The Lion of Belfort.'

Darcy grinned. 'How are you getting on with her?'

'She makes good coffee. And the rum appears in record time.'

'We might have a name, Patron.'

'On the bank job? If he's got his cut he'll be on the way to somewhere like Paraguay by now. Better have the airports and seaports watched. Try Cape Canaveral. He's probably gone into outer space. All sorts of people get up there these days. Who is he?'

'Type called Dufrenic. Josip Dufrenic. Born Budapest. He's a Hungarian but he's lived in France since 1956. I spent half the night checking the names on that list of sewerage workers we got from Benoist. I didn't find much. Just one – this Dufrenic. He has a record. From Reims. Another bank job.'

'Sounds a possible customer. Where is he now?'

Darcy grimaced. 'Not around here,' he said. 'He's lying in a coffin in the Cimetière de Pejoces. He died in November.'

Pel and Darcy ate lunch at a brasserie in the Rue de Tivoli. They hadn't tried it before and decided not to again. The knives were blunt, the wine seemed to be suffering from metal fatigue and the rest of the meal tasted as if it had come direct from the freezer.

'It's the preservatives,' Pel said irritably. 'They stick so much in these days, there's no need to embalm you when you die. It's a plot by the undertakers.'

As they talked, outside a dog lifted its leg against a lamp post. It seemed to symbolize their lack of success.

The bank job seemed to have reached a stalemate and Pel knew the investigation wasn't moving ahead at all. Whoever had done it had planned it well and they'd kept their mouths shut. There hadn't been a murmur from

105

anywhere except Meluc's wife despite the fact that everybody had their ears to the ground and all the informers had been tapped. He had come to a dead stop.

Morell, who had been put on the Sobelec television and video theft case, hadn't come up with anything yet either. The only movement they'd seen was in the assault and battery and making an affray case at Bezay involving the circus twin, Georges Guillet. The fight in the bar that had brought him a broken ankle and a place in the hospital at Chatillon. But it had also alerted the police to him – and interest had begun over an accusation that he was the driver of a car stolen in Gray which had been used during a breaking and entering at Fontaine. There was still also the threat that his brother would try to spirit him away from the cop who was watching his hospital room.

'I sent the Lion of Belfort to make enquiries,' Darcy said. 'Nice easy job for her. It'll enable her to get her bearings.'

As Pel and Darcy regarded the remains of their meal with disgust, Annie was doing just as Darcy had suggested and was getting her bearings.

Her task was made more difficult because of continued snow. Bezay was to the north in an area of sharp hills and hidden valleys and the roads were blurred and the signs plastered with white. Since it had begun to seem that Guillet was indeed the driver of the car in question, Annie started her enquiries with a call on the owner of the circus that had employed him.

It was cold and the shabby little group of caravans stood outside the big top under the leaden skies, placarded by an elaborate notice proclaiming it in huge nineteenth-century curlicue letters to be Malmette's Magnificent Circus.

She found the owner in the tent frustratedly trying to school an unwilling pony. The owner was a woman, Euphemia Malmette, as wide as she was high, with a foreign voice to rival Bardolle's and a set of gold teeth that looked as if they'd come direct from the vaults of the Banque de France.

'*Move*, you son of a pig,' she was roaring at the circling animal. She gestured at Annie. 'The stupid bastard jumps every time I crack the bloody whip,' she complained. 'It's only for show and to make a nice noise but if the customers think I'm being cruel, it's not much good, is it? I haven't touched the sod yet.'

Annie introduced herself and explained her enquiry.

'Oh, well,' Euphemia Malmette said. 'Circus folk are a bit different from other people, aren't they? It's the life they lead. The Guillets are smart and agile and do a good act. Pretending to be one man in two places at once. Identical twins, see. But I wouldn't say they're the straightest in the world. Quite a lot of 'em aren't. Get on, you bugger,' she yelled at the horse. It rolled its eyes and seemed to wince at the noise.

'It's easy to get away with something when you're on the road,' Euphemia Malmette went on. 'You're hard to catch up with. And those two are devoted to each other. Twins are like that. So are circus folk. We're not part of the ordinary community – never have been. No settled home, see? We're on the move all the time. Some do lift things occasionally. I bet Georges did. He's a bit light-fingered. Had one or two things of mine. Will he go to gaol?'

'If he has a record he might,' Annie said.

'I think he has.' Madame Malmette shrugged. 'Oh, well. The circus will always use their act. He can come back when he's paid his fine or done his stretch or whatever they give him. What we'll do with François, his twin brother, when he turns up, though, I don't know. He won't settle easy. Circus folk are like that. It's the life they lead.'

Annie found the proprietor of the bar at Bezay who, it turned out, was the man who claimed the car was his, sitting behind the zinc watching his wife do the work. He had a fractured jaw and was looking sorry for himself.

'It's not a bad fracture,' he mumbled through the bandages. 'He got me when I wasn't looking. I'm glad the saucy little sod got a broken ankle.'

'Did you break it?' Annie asked.

'No. I'd have been glad to, though. I was fond of that car. He drove up here as smooth as you like. Didn't know it came from here, see. He did the ankle himself trying to jump over a table to get away. It overbalanced and down he went. Perhaps he was trying to do a death-defying leap. They say he's a tumbler or something in a circus and that's what they do, isn't it?'

'Well, if it is,' Annie said, 'he obviously needs a bit of practice.'

She decided it might be a good idea to visit the hospital and have a talk with the accused man, but she arrived at an inopportune moment.

'Give him a minute or two,' the nurse said. 'His twin brother, François, has just come in to see him.'

'He's turned up?'

'Has he been missing? Anyway, he's here and it'll be lunch time in a few minutes. He's also injured his foot and he's on crutches. It's sprained, he says, and his doctor's put a tight bandage on it. He looks just like our Guillet. It's amazing about twins, isn't it? They not only look alike, they think alike, and even injure their ankles alike.'

'It's the life they lead,' Annie said.

Growing impatient, she headed up the stairs to the second floor where Georges Guillet was in his single room. A soporific policeman was sitting on a chair outside. As she arrived, so did the meals trolley, pushed from the lift by a civilian worker, an elderly woman in a checked overall. And just at the same time, the man she assumed was François Guillet emerged from the room where his brother, Georges, was in bed.

He nodded to the policeman and set off down the corridor on his crutches. It was then that Annie noticed that he wore plaster and not bandages and it dawned on her that he wasn't the man the nurse had noticed coming in on a visit but was the man *she* had come to see. The man she was looking at was Georges Guillet himself and the man lying in his bed was his brother François, ready, Annie had no doubt, to make a bolt for it as soon as the prisoner had walked out in his place. As they were twins, it wasn't a difficult act to work. According to Madame Malmette, they did it at every performance of Malmette's Magnificent Circus.

She yelled for help and started to run, backed up by the cop from outside the room who almost immediately went down to a swing from the crutch. Annie herself just missed a skull fracture.

Then the brother, François, his bandages half stripped off and agile as a performing monkey, appeared at a run from the room where the prisoner had been. The nurse was at the end of the corridor, screaming her head off, the cop lying unconscious at her feet. Annie was dazed from her near escape and the two brothers were bolting for the stairs, the one with his foot in plaster hoisted across the back of the other who was scuttling along trailing three metres of bandage. All Annie could think of doing was to grab the lunch trolley.

'That's the patients' lunches!' roared the auxiliary.

Ignoring her, Annie swung the trolley round, sending the covered plates balanced on top flying in all directions to spatter the walls with soup and fruit tart. With a good hard shove, she sent the conveyance, along with the

109

dozen lunches it contained, flying along the corridor. It shot down the stairs with the noise of a pile-up on the N7. With it went the Guillet twins.

They didn't lose their prisoner. In fact, they gained one, with a matching broken ankle.

'It's being twins,' Annie told Pel.

'The hospital's demanding an apology,' Darcy reported with a broad grin. 'Probably even compensation. They say Annie's thrown the whole place into confusion. She's wrecked the meals trolley for the Auguste Beaumarchais Ward, ruined eighteen lunches, deprived the patients of their food, spattered the walls with soup and blackcurrant tart so that they'll need redecorating, broken a visitor's ankle, given the civilian helper hysterics and set the whole of the Auguste Beaumarchais Ward in an uproar from which it isn't expected to recover in a hurry.'

'Don't see their problems,' said Pel calmly. 'A cop's been knocked unconscious, and it's our job to stop villains escaping. Besides, haven't they picked up another customer? What are they complaining about? But what about the Lion of Belfort?'

'She's come out of it with nothing worse than a black eye. She showed brains and initiative. Courage, too. She's quite a girl, isn't she?'

'I'd say she was a one-man demolition squad. I suppose she deserves a commendation in her file,' replied Pel drily.

'Well,' Darcy said, 'it wasn't a bad effort for her first week or two in a new job.'

Misset was all too quick to offer congratulations. 'That's quite a black eye you've got.'

But Annie wasn't taken in by his smooth talk. 'There's

one waiting for you, too,' she pointed out, 'if you try to lay a hand on me.'

Suddenly Morell was making progress. He had been going round all the shops in the city that sold videos and televisions on the understanding that if the culprits of the Sobelec theft had been boys, as he suspected, they might have made a few enquiries beforehand. Including the major stores and the Nouvelles Galeries there were quite a number, but he struck gold eventually.

'They came here,' the manager of the radio and television department of the Nouvelles Galeries said. 'It must have been them. There were two of them and they were asking a lot of questions about prices and so on. They seemed interested in the videos and the computers, and they were the right age.'

'Have you a description?'

'One had red hair. He was tall. In the way kids of sixteen are tall. All arms and legs and neck. No breadth. The other seemed to be the leader. He was shortish and slight and wore two ear-rings in his left ear. Why do they do it?'

'Because they want to raise money,' Morell said.

'No, not steal. Wear ear-rings.'

'Oh.' Morell grinned. 'Isn't it supposed to stop headaches? Or stop you going cross-eyed?'

Morell knew he must now go to the College of Art to find out if they had a student who was tall and gangling with red hair, or one who was short and slight and wore two ear-rings in his left ear to stop him going cross-eyed. Unfortunately they hadn't.

Morell sighed for he realized he would now have to visit every senior school in the area and talk to the art masters. Morell didn't fancy the idea, especially with the

111

snow that persisted in lying about like somebody's dirty linen.

There were several schools within easy reach of the Nouvelles Galeries, more still if you went into the districts round the city, and it meant visiting them all.

Morell finally found what he was looking for at the Lycée St Julien.

'Yes, we have boys well capable of manufacturing disabled stickers,' the art master agreed. 'They're not very difficult – just that wheelchair logo and a bit of lettering. All they'd have to do would be get the right colour paper.' He smiled indulgently. 'They probably got it here, even. We carry all colours. With a bit of care I could do it myself and I'm only a teacher of drawing without the cunning of these young bastards.'

'I'm looking for two of them,' Morell said. 'One tall and gangling with red hair. One dark, shorter and wearing two ear-rings in his left ear.'

'Guy Loisel,' the art master said immediately. 'And René Carrera. Loisel's the tall one. Carrera's been forbidden to wear the ear-rings at school. He's too big for his boots and too old for his years. They're always together. They're cousins. Have they been up to something?'

'You bet your life they have,' Morell said. 'Stealing.'

The art master whistled. 'I wouldn't put it past them,' he admitted. 'They're a bit of a trial and they're always in trouble. Bad homes, I suppose. The sad thing is that both of them have ability and if they'd only try they'd both get decent jobs. But they never will. It's their background. They come from the Arsenal area.'

'Are they at school now?'

'I'm afraid not. They often aren't. This time they haven't been for several days.'

Morell wasn't surprised. 'I'd better have their addresses,' he said with a sigh. More leg work, he thought.

10

Pel had a small stroke of luck the following day when a man walking his dog found a protective helmet in a ditch outside Messigny. It was in the grass by the side of the road leading north out of the city towards the Plateau de Langres, made of tough plastic, with fittings inside to hold it in place on the head, and was coloured orange.

The finder remembered reading somewhere that the men who had robbed the Crédit Rural bank had climbed out of a manhole wearing orange protective helmets. Duty clashed with self-interest but in the end duty won and he took the helmet he had found to the police at Fontaine.

The *sous-brigadier* in charge of the substation recognized its significance at once and ran him in his little cream van down to the Hôtel de Police. There were no fingerprints but it was a minuscule step forward, and Pel needed cheering up.

'It seems', Pel said, 'to indicate that it was abandoned as they bolted out of the city.'

'And', Darcy added, 'that we know at last which way they bolted – north towards Chatillon or Langres.'

Darcy arranged for the local radio station to mention the trophy on their evening news and the following day another orange helmet was brought in. A tractor driver had found it on the edge of one of the fields he was working and had thought it suited him so well he had been wearing it for several days.

'Where did you find it?' Pel asked.

'Where I work.'

'Where's that?'

'In the fields round Baignay-les-Jeufs.'

Again there were no fingerprints, which indicated that the bank robbers had continued to be careful, and no more protective helmets turned up in spite of the fact that all substations were told to keep their eyes open. The local radio station mentioned the helmets two or three times then dropped them as being no longer of news value. Pel wasn't surprised. You could blow up bridges over the Seine in Paris and it would hold the attention for a day or two until something else happened then it would be forgotten.

'At least', he said, 'it indicates they ran for the high ground. It's lonely up there round Baignay and Messigny. They've probably got some hide-out arranged where they've hidden the loot.'

It was obvious that one of the gang had tossed his helmet away in a spirit of *joie de vivre*, of something accomplished, something done, and a second had followed suit. Then one of the others had realized that an orange protective helmet was a clue and no more had been cast aside. If it indicated the direction they'd taken as they'd fled from the scene of the crime, it didn't indicate much more. Every cop in the triangle north of the city between Chatillon and Langres was told to keep his eyes open but the items on the radio news not only had the effect of alerting people to be on the look-out, they also warned the gang. Pel knew there'd be no more protective helmets leading in a straight line to the hide-out.

Pel and Darcy then began to check the staff at Crédit Rural again, but, as Gilbaud, the manager, had said, none of them had been noticed particularly looking around the stationery store. The most likely suspect seemed to be the junior clerk, who was the dogsbody, runner of errands and the one who was always sent to the store cupboard to replenish forms, carbons and paper. He was a fat, pink boy who blushed every time they spoke to him and they ruled him out at once.

With the snow, Pel decided to leave for home in reasonable time. The roads were dreadful and the sky was still heavy with cloud. When he arrived, Yves Pasquier from next door was sitting at the kitchen table in front of a plate littered with crumbs.

'I've come for my slice of cake,' he said, with his mouth full. 'It's late and I almost forgot.'

It had surprised Pel to discover that Madame Routy had a soft spot for the boy. Somewhere in that agate organ she called a heart there were clearly portions that still had warmth in them. She regularly baked cakes of surprising quality and since neither Pel nor his wife ate cake, he could only assume she did it for no other reason than to give it away in doorstep slices to Yves Pasquier.

'Cake's bad for you,' he said.

He put on his severe expression but in fact he was always pleased to see Yves Pasquier. Although the typists and newly joined cops at the Hôtel de Police considered him a walking Reign of Terror, he had a surprisingly soft spot for small boys.

'I think it's going to snow again,' Yves said, swallowing the last large piece of cake with effort. 'Snow stops everything.'

Pel nodded. Even his circulation, he thought.

'Have you caught those bank robbers yet?'

'Not yet.'

'You will.'

Pel wished he had Yves Pasquier's faith.

The conversation took a turn towards the bizarre. 'I'm going to be a frog,' Yves said.

Pel's eyebrows rose. 'And be kissed by a princess so that you turn into a prince?'

The boy gave him the sort of look all small boys give their elders when they think they're being patronized.

'Is it a play?' Pel asked.

'I think so. At school. I'm not sure. I don't really know what's going on.'

Neither, thought Pel, remembering his own early days at school, had he.

'It's for the end of term. They're going to paint my face green and yellow. It's about animals having a party. I'd rather be a knight or a pirate or something from outer space.' An indignant note crept in. 'Why do lady teachers always make you dress up as animals?'

It was something Pel remembered with disgust from his own childhood. 'Domination,' he replied. 'Or maybe they get tired of looking at you.'

'Antoine Gilbert's mother's got rats,' Yves said.

'In the play?'

'No. At home.'

'White rats?'

'I think they're ordinary brown ones.'

'Who's Antoine Gilbert?'

'He's my friend. Have you got many friends, Monsieur Pel?'

'No.' Pel considered it a triumph of skill and management.

'Don't you like people?'

It was a difficult question and Pel didn't want to be accused of corrupting minors. He tried to be honest. 'Not much,' he said. 'Just Madame Pel. And you.'

Yves smiled proudly. 'Antoine's going to be a fox,' he said. 'He sits in front of me at school. He passes bits of

116

paper with answers on them to me. Under the seat. I give him sweets.'

Criminality, Pel decided, was spreading. The world was full of crooks and shysters. Even the village school.

He tried to be polite. 'How's she got rats?'

'She feeds the birds.'

'You should never feed birds in the country,' Pel said solemnly. 'You should make them work for a living. There's plenty around for them. They've only got to look for it.'

'She likes birds. She's into being Green. She's soppy about them. That's why she feeds them. Then the rats come. We once had rats. Before we came to live here. We had chickens and kept the chicken feed in a hut. It had a wooden floor and the rats came through the holes in the planking for it. When Pappy pulled the hut down there were rats' nests all over.'

'Did you see them?'

'No. I wasn't born then.'

'Oh.' It was time, Pel considered, to bring the conversation to a close. He was tired and hungry and he needed a drink. 'I'll have to be going,' he said.

'That's all right,' Yves said. 'So will I.'

As the door closed behind him, Madame Pel appeared from upstairs. She kissed Pel and headed for the drinks cupboard.

'Next door's son and heir's eating us out of house and home,' Pel observed mildly.

'Oh, that's normal enough,' she said. 'He does it every day.'

'Can't they afford to feed him?'

'They probably need help. Small boys eat a lot. They have hollow legs, I believe.'

'He's going to be a frog. In a play.'

'Yes.' Madame had her head in the cupboard searching for bottles and glasses. 'I offered to help them with the make-up. I used to be good at it.'

They went into the salon. Mahler was being exhilarating on the record player but Madame turned him off hurriedly. She'd discovered that Mahler wasn't conducive to good temper in her husband, who couldn't tell a tune from a warthog. Though he was prepared for her sake to sit through a few of the more melodious bits of opera, he'd never had much time for Mahler. She poured him a whisky.

'Are you making any progress?' she asked.

'No,' Pel said.

'What will they do with the money? They surely won't be able to spend it.'

'They could. It's all old notes. Jewellery will disappear to Paris or Marseilles, I expect. But they'll have to be careful. We're keeping a sharp look-out. Somebody will slip up eventually.'

'By spending too much?'

'I doubt it. Overspending and not being careful was what caught those GB train robbers. They'll leave it alone for a long time, just spending a little here and there. They might even use it to finance something else so that in the end we'll be searching for two lots of loot.'

She nodded and yawned. Time to stop talking shop. Or Pel's shop at least.

While Pel's investigation was proceeding at a minimal pace, Nosjean was suddenly having success beyond his wildest dreams.

He hadn't ever expected to turn up Colette Esterhazy again. A girl who was as clever as she was, as beautiful, as kind, as friendly, a girl who seemed to pick up admirers as a sheep in a hedgerow picked up burrs, would surely be at the other side of the world in the time it took

118

to snap your fingers. She had with her two pictures worth over a million francs, which, as he well knew from what Mijo had told him, could easily be disguised as something less interesting and less valuable to get an export licence. With those she could live for some time. And with the skill she had, surely she could set herself up in some place like New York, Berlin, London, Madrid, and become an established painter under a false name? With the looks and charm she quite clearly possessed she could even end up marrying a Californian millionaire and in no time be living it up in San Francisco or somewhere like that.

Not for a minute did he expect to find her quickly but he had reckoned without the way men notice pretty girls. Thinking about it later, he realized a girl like Colette Esterhazy couldn't hide. She was too beautiful, too charming.

With Mijo's help he had warned dealers to be on the look-out. He had heard a whisper even that the pictures had been seen in Paris and had got in touch with the Art Dealers' Association and told them he expected their full co-operation. They usually gave it under such circumstances because, when a warning of that sort was put out, it didn't pay to handle anything even faintly fishy. To his surprise, within a few days he received a telephone call from Toulouse. Dealers were inclined to be secretive about their moves but the suggestion that a thief was involved always put them on the alert. They were not against selling something doubtful but where a charge of handling stolen goods was possible, they preferred to back off. The dealer in Toulouse, by the name of Maxime Havard, had had a Douanier Rousseau offered him two days before.

'A Rousseau isn't all that common,' he explained. 'He didn't paint all that many and one offered by a beautiful woman stands in the memory.'

'Did she give a name?' Nosjean asked.

'Yes. Angelique Leroux, with an address in Albi. I don't think either was genuine because she had a bag with her with the initials C.E. on it and an old airport label which gave a different address in Beauvais.' Havard had obviously been suspicious and, knowing the police were interested, had decided to take no chances.

'Albi being the home town of Toulouse Lautrec and a bit paintable round the cathedral,' he said, 'it seems to breed artists and dealers like bad habits breed mice but I was still a bit startled by the offer when she mentioned that she might also be able to produce a Paot if I were interested. I was told you're looking for a Rousseau and a Paot. The Rousseau's *A Scene Near Enghien*, she said. The Paot's a woodland glade with lots of reds, yellows and blues. Ring a bell?'

'They certainly do. Is she coming back?'

'I persuaded her to come with the pictures tomorrow afternoon. I expect you'll want to be here.'

It didn't take long to persuade Pel to give permission for the journey to Toulouse.

'I've found the paintings, Patron,' Nosjean told him on the phone and during the night he roared down the motorway, driving like a maniac.

Havard's shop was situated close to the Basilica of St Sernin whose Romanesque architecture could be seen from the window. Havard was looking indignant. 'She's not coming,' he said. 'She rang first thing this morning to say she'd found another buyer. She said she was leaving Albi.'

Nosjean frowned. 'Where for?'

'She didn't say.'

Nosjean's enquiries led him nowhere and he set off home in a bad temper. He decided to try Colette Esterhazy's old apartment. It was just possible that someone there might know of some other address she'd mentioned where she might possibly be hiding out.

The door was opened by the daughter, Eloise Sadon. Through her glasses, her eyes shone with excitement. 'But she's *here*,' she said. 'She came back.'

'What?' Nosjean was amazed. 'When did she come?'

'Last night. She seemed upset. I think she's been crossed in love. There was certainly a man in her life. I know that. I think he's let her down.' She had clearly been raised on copies of *True Romance*.

He set off up the stairs at a run. There were a lot of them and he was panting as he reached the top, still unable to believe in his good fortune, and knocked on the door of the studio. There was no reply so he tried the door. It was unlocked and he eased it open slowly.

Colette Esterhazy was sitting on a low stool. He knew at once it was her. He'd never met her but there couldn't be two women as beautiful as she was. She lifted her head as he appeared and he knew at once why it was that Eloise Sadon had such a crush on her, why men like Distaing, Lepic and Leygues had been putty in her hands. She was one of the most striking women he'd ever seen. He'd gone through the usual crushes himself, moving from Brigitte Bardot to Charlotte Rampling to Catherine Deneuve. He'd been in love with them all and, taking them as his standard, he'd fallen in love with a whole series of girls who'd looked like one or another. He'd even been in the habit of classifying girls – as astrologers classified their subjects: an Aries, a Pisces, et cetera – as Deneuves, Ramplings or Bardots. Mijo Lehmann was a Rampling as Colette Esterhazy was a Deneuve. He realized that, but for Mijo Lehmann, he could just as easily fall in love with Colette Esterhazy.

Her features were exact and her nose was small and straight. Her mouth and chin were wonderfully chiselled and she had that great gift of God, huge brown eyes with naturally blonde hair. And when she stood up he saw her figure was as near perfect as it could be.

He sighed.

She looked straight at him and he could see she had been weeping. Unlike most girls, however, weeping didn't seem to detract from her looks. Almost the contrary.

'Colette Esterhazy?' he asked, though he knew the question was pointless. She was quite obviously Colette Esterhazy.

She nodded. 'Yes,' she said and her voice was as good as the rest of her, low and melodious.

'I think we need to talk.' Nosjean flipped open his identity card with its red, white and blue stripes. 'I'm Jean-Luc Nosjean. Sergeant. Brigade Criminelle.' He didn't know why he gave her his full name. He didn't normally when faced with wrongdoers. It just seemed to make things gentler and he had a feeling he needed to be gentle. 'I have good reason to believe you have here two pictures, one a Rousseau, one a Paot, the property of the Musée des Arts Modernes.'

She gazed at him with her huge eyes. 'No,' she whispered. 'They're not here.'

'They're not?' Nosjean's heart sank. He looked about him. Beyond the girl and the small overnight bag alongside her, there was nothing more in the room than there had been when he had last seen it. 'Then where are they?'

'I haven't got them.'

'That seems clear. But you had them the day before yesterday. You offered them to a dealer called Havard in Toulouse.'

'Yes. But I haven't got them now.'

'Why did you break your appointment to take them to him?'

'Because I hadn't got the pictures any more.'

'So where are they?'

'I . . .' She paused. 'He said . . .'

'Who said?'

'He's a friend.' She sighed. 'That's all. Just a friend.'

'And what *did* he say?'

'I . . .' She paused again. 'I can't tell you.'

'Has *he* got the pictures?'

'I can't say.'

'Why not?'

She didn't answer.

'Did you let this friend have the pictures?'

'I . . . I suppose so.'

'Who is he?'

'I can't tell you that.'

'You were hoping to sell the pictures, weren't you? To Havard.'

'Yes.'

'Why did you change your mind?'

'He said . . .'

'Who said? This friend?'

'Yes.'

'Well, come on. What did he say?'

'I . . . I've forgotten.'

'Why did you come back here?'

'I've nowhere else to go.'

'I think you'll have to accompany me to the Hôtel de Police. Do you realize that?'

Her expression was so forlorn Nosjean felt a brute. 'Yes,' was all she replied.

'I've got a car. You'd better bring your bag.' In addition to her personal belongings there might be an address book, a letter, something to indicate the identity of the friend who, Nosjean was certain by this time, had the missing pictures. She nodded and picked up the bag.

'It's not much. Have you nothing else?'

'Not here,' she said. 'They're all at my friend's.'

'Hadn't we better go and collect them?'

She was too clever to fall for that. 'No,' she said. 'I'll manage.'

As they walked to the car, followed by the agonized eyes of Eloise Sadon, Nosjean found he was carrying the bag for her. She gave him no trouble but walked quietly alongside. As he unlocked the car, she climbed into the front passenger seat and sat silently.

'You did take those pictures from the Musée des Arts Modernes, didn't you?' Nosjean asked as he climbed in beside her, very conscious of her presence and the perfume she wore.

'Yes,' she said. 'I took them.'

'Why?'

'Because ... I ... he said ...' She stopped. 'I don't know.'

There was obviously a story behind the theft and Nosjean was intrigued to find out what it was. He felt he was in the presence of a tremendous personal tragedy, small enough against the evil that existed in the world but to this girl clearly world-shattering in its importance. She was shocked, broken, disillusioned by treachery, but she could offer nothing in exchange except loyalty. She was saying nothing.

'You realize you could go to prison, don't you?'

She gave him a frightened look that touched his heart. 'Prison?'

'You've committed a felony. You stole two pictures worth a great deal of money. Did you know they were worth a lot?'

'Oh yes,' she whispered. 'I knew.'

'Where are they now?'

She studied him for a moment, then she shook her head and looked away. 'I can't say,' she repeated.

When Pel returned to his office an exhausted Nosjean was waiting for him. He looked worried.

'Let's have it, *mon brave*,' Pel said.

'I've picked up Colette Esterhazy,' Nosjean reported.

'And the pictures?'

'She hasn't got them. I've just brought her in. I think she's been made a sucker by some type she was in love with.'

'It happens.' Pel spoke from experience. He'd been made a sucker by girls many times in his youth and he still remembered the inadequacy he had felt.

'She was obviously persuaded to make the copies as a means of walking away with the originals. Or else she just happened to be making the copies and was persuaded to switch them.'

'Either way, she still walked away with them.'

Nosjean sighed. 'Yes.'

Pel eyed him sideways. He'd known Nosjean a long time, from the days when he'd been a nervous young cop bleating about his expenses and not having enough time off. He'd grown up a lot since then but there was still a part of him that hadn't changed much. He could have been a marvellous cop but for that. Pel remembered the procession of Nosjean's girl-friends and the crushes he'd had.

'I hear she's very beautiful,' he murmured.

'She is, Patron.' Nosjean paused. 'And from what I've learned about her, the rest of her goes with it. Everybody likes her – even women. Men fall for her. She's kind, gentle, clever – all the rest. And a bit disingenuous. I think she's had a raw deal and I'm wondering if I can't make it a bit easier for her.'

'The law won't look at it that way, *mon brave*.'

'No,' Nosjean agreed. 'But I'd like to find the type behind it. I might, if only I could persuade her to give me his name.'

Pel nodded. But he wondered how difficult Nosjean was going to find that.

11

The weather grew colder and more snow came so that the city looked pretty under its white mantle. It was an old city of solemn buildings and odd angles that belonged to the Middle Ages so that you tended as you rounded a corner to expect a woman in a wimple or a man in coloured hose carrying a sword. It was known as the city of a hundred belfries but at the moment the bells sounding for Mass sounded eerily muffled and anybody in wimples and coloured hose would also have needed to wear fur hats and galoshes.

There was a partial thaw and a sprinkle of rain, then finally the frost came down, solid and hard.

Because much of the country was surrounded by sea, the climate of France was normally temperate. The summers were gentle as a rule and, apart from in the Alps, the Pyrenees and the mountainous areas of the Massif Central, the winters were not usually harsh. Every now and then, however, maverick conditions occurred and when they did so at the end of the year the weather came straight from the Russian Arctic. This year was an example.

Under leaden skies, cars skated about and refused to start in the morning. Motor-cycles slipped from between their riders' legs as they turned corners. Plumbers found themselves in great demand as pipes were blocked solid with ice, and house owners trying to thaw them out found water coming through ceilings and under doors. And, incredibly, for the first time in years the canal froze: good, solid, thick ice that brought the barges to a standstill, roped alongside each other, the iron chimneys protruding from their cabin roofs red-hot with the stoking of the stove in the cabin below.

Nosjean was still trying to get Svengali's name from Colette Esterhazy. She was in the women's wing of 72, Rue d'Auxonne and it was obvious her charm had worked on her gaolers. She had been given one of the better cells and was left alone.

'She does what she has to do without complaint,' the Matron told Nosjean. 'She tidies her cell and keeps herself clean. She's even a help in some ways because she asked if she could have a sketching pad and she entertains some of the other women by drawing their faces. Half of them have their portraits hanging up in their cells now. She's good.'

'Given a chance,' Nosjean said feelingly, 'I think she could one day be great.'

Despite his sympathy, however, he got nowhere with the girl. 'Look,' he said, 'why protect this man? He's got you into a whole heap of trouble. Let's have his name and we'll pick him up. He deserves to be where you are.'

'What will they do to me?'

Nosjean suspected that when she appeared before the magistrates, she'd have the same effect on the red-robed splendour on the bench that she had on him and everyone else. They'd be influenced by her simplicity and her beauty, as he was, as her landlady, her landlady's daughter, Distaing, Leygues, everybody, had been, and deal leniently with her. After that, if she could only forget the bastard who'd led her astray, there was every chance she could pick up where she had left off.

But it had obviously caused her suffering and Nosjean's heart – a very soft heart where pretty women were concerned – bled for her.

'All we want is a name,' he said.

'I can't give you one,' she insisted.

'You know his name?'

'Oh, yes. I know his name.'

'Did you live together?'

'On and off.'

'Where?'

'I can't tell you.'

'In this city?'

'No. Not here.'

Well, Nosjean thought, he couldn't search the whole of France without some sort of lead. He tried again with mounting desperation.

'Don't you see what he's done to you? Landed you in gaol – with the possibility of a long sentence.' However, he didn't believe this for a minute. Magistrates were as human as anybody else and they would doubtless read her a lecture, put her on probation as a first offender, tell her she'd been led on by a wicked, cruel man, and that they were giving her a chance to pull her life together.

'Yes,' she said. 'I see that.'

'Don't you want a little of your own back?'

'No.'

Nosjean could well believe it. He even wondered sometimes if she was as big a crook as her seducer and was keeping quiet because she feared the law of the underworld. But he found it a theory that was hard to accept.

'Just a name,' he urged.

'I can't give you one,' she replied doggedly and Nosjean felt like screaming aloud in frustration.

Morell found his two boys without further difficulty. They lived within fifty metres of each other in the same street, a grubby thoroughfare called the Rue de Bruges. It was a narrow alley with shabby blocks of apartments, even shabbier with the icicles and the iron sky. There was no sign of them or their parents at their homes but neighbours told him of their whereabouts.

'They'll be with their grandmother,' they said. 'She lives near the Rue de Rouen.'

Despite the cold, there was a conference of aproned women in the street and between them they worked out the address. 'Apartment 6a, Rue Alphonse Bordier, 17.'

The Rue Alphonse Bordier was another street like the Rue de Bruges. Narrow, ugly and devoid of hope. Morell wondered who Alphonse Bordier was. The builder? The builder's son? Some French hero? Some half-baked politician? The French had always had a liking for calling streets after their heroes. After all, they could hardly call them after their swindlers, murderers, thieves. Rue Landru. Rue Stavinsky. Rue Robespierre. It wouldn't work. Sometimes even the heroes turned out to be anything but heroes and then there had to be a hurried rechristening. Calling streets after people, he decided, carried an inbuilt problem.

Number 17 was a narrow-gutted house, and Apartment 6a was even worse. It consisted of two or three tiny rooms, had clearly once been part of a larger apartment and was as cold as a tomb despite the electric fire that was burning.

The two boys were there, with an old lady who looked about ninety. She sat huddled in a chair, holding a walking stick and staring with blank opaque eyes and no sign of interest at a television which was showing *Pinocchio* in full colour and volume. One of the boys, Loisel, was adjusting the set and, as he entered, Morell heard him ask, 'Can you see that better, Grandmère?' The old lady gave no indication of having heard. The other boy emerged from a tiny cubicle which did duty as a kitchen. He was holding a fork and Morell could smell cooking.

They looked at Morell with trepidation. 'Are you the school inspector?' Loisel asked.

'No,' Morell said. 'I'm a cop.'

There was a long silence.

He showed them his identity card and looked about him. The television set was new and alongside it, connected up, was a video. It was showing 'Play' and what the old lady was looking at was obviously a recording of the film they'd made. Alongside was a pile of video cassettes.

'That came from Sobelec, didn't it?' Morell asked.

Loisel nodded dutifully and Morell knew this was going to be easier than he had thought.

'The video too?' He probed gently.

Another dutiful nod.

'And all the cassettes?'

'Yes.'

'You didn't think you could get away with them, did you?'

The two boys said nothing.

'Why did you steal them? For the old lady?'

'Well,' Carrera said with sudden openness, 'she can't walk much and she lives alone. She's my grandmother. She's his too. We're cousins. We thought we'd try to do something for her.'

'Such as stealing a television?'

'It was for her, not us.'

'Couldn't your parents have bought her one?'

'I don't think they could afford to.'

They told him a long story about both sets of parents having to work, one mother at the station bar, the other in the canteen at Métaux de Bourgogne. Both fathers had unimportant, ill-paid jobs, one as a cook at the barracks, one as a labourer. Carrera did all the talking. A sharp-eyed boy of fifteen, he was obviously brighter than his cousin.

'They haven't got a lot to spare,' he insisted. 'I've got four brothers. He's got three sisters and two brothers. When we're at school Grandmère's on her own. It's rotten being on your own when you don't see and hear things so well. And she likes the pictures. It's something moving. Anything's better than looking at a blank wall all day. When she's alone nothing moves. Nothing. It's like being in a box. A cold box.'

Morell had to admit that what he said was true. He tried to be gentle.

'Couldn't you have managed to afford a black and white television?'

'It's not the same. That's like old photos. Colour's for real.'

'So you stole the television for her?'

'Yes.'

'And the video games?'

'They were for us. We thought we needed a bit of entertainment, too.'

'Couldn't the old lady live with one of the families?'

'There isn't room.'

Morell could well believe it. French families – all good Catholic families, for that matter – took their duties seriously and old people were never abandoned. But there were problems when the houses were small and the families big.

'You were a bit clumsy, weren't you?' he said. 'It didn't take many enquiries to get your names. And what about the car? Where did you get that?'

'It's my father's. Everybody was at work. They share cars to save money and it was his father's turn to drive.'

'You know you're not old enough to drive a car.'

'I've driven it often.' There was a trace of pride and defiance in the reply.

'On the streets?'

'At night.'

'Where did you get the disabled badge?'

'We copied it from one Eddie Detaigne lent us. His father lost a leg at work.'

'Why not use Eddie Detaigne's father's badge?'

'We thought of it but then we thought it might be a good idea to have one of our own.'

'So you could do other jobs like this one?'

'Yes.' Carrera looked at Loisel. 'But that stupid con dropped it somewhere.'

'I know. I picked it up. It's a pity you don't use your skill for something better.'

They probably would, of course, given time, Morell thought. Forging bank notes, for instance.

'It's a good job you've been stopped, isn't it?' he went on. 'That makes about four offences you're guilty of already. Taking a car without consent of the owner. Driving a car without a licence and therefore without insurance. Improperly using a disabled person's badge. Theft. You're in a mess.'

'Will they send us to prison?'

Morell decided that perhaps they wouldn't under the circumstances, especially when he recited the story of the old lady they were trying to help. But it wouldn't do to give them any false hopes. It was better they should shake in their shoes a little.

'I wouldn't like to say,' he admitted. 'The magistrates take a dim view of theft – and a dimmer view of false representation and driving a car without a licence. If you'd hit someone you'd have been in real trouble.' The silence lengthened and Morell tried to stop himself feeling sorry for them. He failed. 'All right, you'd better

133

come with me. What are we going to do about the old lady?'

'She'll be all right,' Loisel said. 'We'll give her some grub and this video's nearly finished. We can put another one in if you can wait a bit and by the time that finishes the next-door neighbour will be back. She'll look in. She always does. She won't be any trouble.'

But there were tears in the boys' eyes.

12

Nosjean hadn't given up although he was somewhat depressed. He was determined to find the man behind Colette Esterhazy's downfall and it became almost an obsession, to the point when Mijo Lehmann grew worried.

'It's nothing,' he insisted.

'Have you fallen for her or something?'

'No.' He kissed her. 'It's not that. It's just that I can't stand seeing someone put on a girl who's decent, clever, kindly...'

'And beautiful.'

Nosjean nodded. 'That, too,' he admitted. 'But it's obvious she's not a villain. Everybody who's ever met her thinks the world of her. She's good-natured, considerate...'

'And beautiful.' Mijo's voice was growing tart.

'Oh, God,' Nosjean snapped, aware that it was their first quarrel. 'Yes, that. But some sod's had her sent to prison. He persuaded her to steal those pictures and, having got them, he sent her off to Toulouse to see a dealer, then, while she was out of the way, disappeared with them, leaving her to face the music.'

'Are you sure *she* wasn't in on it?'

'I'm sure.'

Mijo shrugged. 'I wish I were,' she said.

Even Mijo's hostility didn't make Nosjean let up. Muffled to the eyebrows, he made enquiries round the University, at Colette Esterhazy's apartment, in the bars she might have visited, the little restaurant near her apartment where she sometimes ate. They all knew her – who wouldn't, he thought, looking as she did. One or two of them had seen a man with her but none of them knew his name. The name 'Patrick' occurred more than once, though, and Nosjean realized with some small triumph that he had at least got part of an identification.

'God,' said Courtrand when Nosjean appeared. 'Are you still at it?'

'Investigations aren't finished in a couple of days,' Nosjean said stiffly. He explained what he was after and Courtrand frowned, not that pleased to be interrupted. There was a girl perched on a stool who was naked but didn't seem at all perturbed to have Nosjean looking at her.

Courtrand stared at him angrily, then he gestured at the girl. 'All right,' he said. 'Put on. Go and make some coffee. And get the rum out. It's cold in here. You'll be needing a drop and so will I.' He put down his palette and brushes and turned to Nosjean. 'Well?'

'Colette Esterhazy.'

'Yes?'

'I want the name of a man she lived with. The man who put her up to this con job. Do you know him?'

'Of course I don't.'

'Did you ever see her with a man?'

'No. Never. Well . . .' Courtrand paused. 'A guy once came to collect her when she'd been sitting for me late.'

'Did she use his name?'

'She called him Patrick. She introduced him. What was it?' Courtrand beat his fist on his forehead. 'She said he was a painter and I asked if I ought to have heard of him.

She said I would in time.' He clicked his fingers. 'I've got it. Patrick Lourdais. I remember because I made a few enquiries about him. He's small time. Makes no money at all. Tell you the truth, I didn't like the look of him.'

'Do you know where he lives?'

'Haven't the foggiest.'

'Didn't she tell you?'

'You don't usually give the address, date of birth, where they were born and why, when you introduce somebody.'

Nosjean left Courtrand's studio as he was yelling, 'All right. Take off. We've got to make up time and my brushes are getting cold.'

At least, Nosjean thought with greater optimism, he had a name now. But Patrick Lourdais was a common enough name and he wouldn't be easy to find.

He began his new enquiries at the University but nobody had ever heard of Patrick Lourdais. He tried Colette Esterhazy's old apartment, which was now occupied by another student, and drew another blank. He tried the bars and restaurants again. He got nowhere. It was, he decided, going to be a long job and one in which he could foresee increasing tensions between himself and Mijo.

He was surprised, therefore, when he discovered exactly where Patrick Lourdais was the very next day.

He was in Paris. And he was dead.

The story was in one of the rags Sarrazin, the freelance journalist, represented. ARTIST SHOT IN LOVE NEST, the headline shrieked. And there, just below, was the name of Patrick Lourdais.

Well, the first thing anybody might have thought, imagined Nosjean, was that Colette Esterhazy had done it. But she couldn't have, could she? Because he hadn't been dead long and she had been in 72, Rue d'Auxonne. The newspaper told a story of a man whose studio was regularly visited by women. That wasn't abnormal for an artist, especially as Lourdais, like Courtrand, had specialized in painting them. But it seemed he was known in the neighbourhood behind Montmartre for his life style and for the pretty girls he was involved with.

Nosjean presented himself to Pel. 'Patron,' he said, 'I think we might be able to recover those two stolen pictures.'

'Again?' He replied cynically.

Nosjean flushed. He showed Pel the story in the newspaper and explained what he had learned. 'That's the type I'm after,' he said. 'I'd like to go to Paris and see the police there. I expect they've got the pictures.'

'If he hasn't sold them,' Pel said drily. 'Judging by this story, he might well have. You need money for the sort of life he lived.'

'Patron,' Nosjean urged, 'you can't get rid of pictures like those in a hurry. They're too well known. They're worth a lot of money.'

Pel gave his reluctant consent. He felt a little bitter. He couldn't see why Nosjean and Morell should have all the luck while the bank hold-up produced so few results. It was an unfair world, he thought.

Nosjean drove the chilly distance over the winter roads to Paris to interview the police of the 18th Arrondissement where Lourdais had had his studio behind the Butte de Montmartre. The countryside looked like the Arctic and Paris was a stark silhouette.

The police weren't able to help much. They did what they could, however, and told him what they knew.

'Shot at close range,' a detective called Regnard explained. 'Belgian .38 pistol.'

138

Pictures were produced. They showed a man lying on his back with a bullet wound in the right temple.

'He didn't do it himself,' Regnard said. 'There were no powder marks worth noticing on his face. The pistol was in his hand. We think it was put there but the only fingerprints on it were his. Classic suicide arrangement but it wasn't suicide. It was murder. Someone came up here. Someone he probably knew because there was no sign of a struggle. We think they sat talking and there were indications they had a drink together. Cigarette ends. Dirty glasses. Fingerprints. But none we know. As though they had discussed business.'

Perhaps they did, Nosjean thought. Business concerning two valuable pictures.

'But then, we think,' Regnard went on, 'the visitor produced a pistol and shot him. Do you know why? Because if you do, we'd like to know too. We're checking other artists and all the shady dealers but we're not getting anywhere.'

Nosjean had no idea why Lourdais was dead, but he guessed it was connected with the stolen pictures.

Regnard had seen no paintings such as Nosjean described and didn't even know who Douanier Rousseau and Gustave Paot were. However, he took him to the sealed studio and allowed him to look round. There were plenty of paintings about, almost all of them women, one that he recognized as Colette Esterhazy. Having learned a little about art from Mijo, Nosjean didn't consider them very good. He went through every canvas but there was no *Scene Near Enghien*, no Paot.

The studio had a decadent look about it. It was grubby and the nude paintings verged on the pornographic. He wasn't quite sure what to do. He didn't fancy going back to Pel and telling him he was unsuccessful once more. He decided to try Colette Esterhazy again. She might know of some place where Lourdais might have hidden the pictures.

She had read of Lourdais' death in the newspaper she was allowed. 'He was shot, wasn't he?' she said as Nosjean stripped off coat and scarf and gloves.

'Yes. Belgian .38. Did you have such a pistol?'

'I didn't do it.'

'You couldn't have. But somebody might have found your pistol and used that.'

'I never had a pistol.' But despite the flat negatives of her answers Colette Esterhazy seemed suddenly willing to talk. Around her in the cell were portraits of other prisoners and one or two that Nosjean recognized as being prison visitors. There was also one of Distaing, the *gardien* at the Musée des Arts Modernes. She had obviously been filling her time.

'They're saying the magistrates might not be too hard on me.' Colette spoke tentatively.

'What will you do when you're free?' asked Nosjean gently, trying to encourage her to think more positively.

'Go south. I want to paint for a while. Then I'll come back and finish my degree. They've told me I'll be allowed to.' At once a certain light came into her eyes and with a shock he realized that this was perhaps how some of the major Impressionists had seen their vocation – in the south. She was a real painter, he thought, maybe she'll be of major importance in the future and when this was all behind her. Suddenly he had the odd feeling of being privileged to be in her company. Then she reached out impulsively and took his hand. 'Everybody's being so kind. I've been talking to them, you see.'

'I wish you'd talk to me,' said Nosjean with irony but he knew that the breakthrough had come.

'I will now he's dead.' Nosjean felt a sense of shock. 'Well, he *is* dead, isn't he? There's no need to remain silent about him any more.'

Nosjean eyed her warily, wondering what was coming. 'I went there,' he said. 'I didn't find the pictures, though. Where would he hide them?'

She shrugged. 'I've no idea.'

'It would be better for you if we could find them. Especially if you were involved,' he said, tightening the screws a little.

But she remained calm. 'I can't. I don't know where they are. I'll tell you everything else but I can't tell you that because I don't know.'

'You picked on a real swine,' Nosjean said with feeling.

She nodded and then stared up at him calmly. 'How many mistakes about people have *you* made, monsieur? None at all? You must be a cold fish. As for me – yes, I have made mistakes, and with him I made a big one. I've realized that almost all of what he told me was untrue – was a complete fantasy.' She looked up at Nosjean, her eyes clear and frank. 'You know, it was Patrick who got me to sleep with Arthur Leygues.'

Nosjean sat bolt upright. He hadn't expected this and he cursed himself for his complacency. 'He did *what*?'

'I didn't want to. But that was how Arthur allowed me to have the pictures out of their frames.'

So Distaing had been right after all, thought Nosjean. 'Did Leygues know about Lourdais?'

'No.' She sounded very positive and yet he wasn't sure if he believed her.

Nosjean was thinking fast, suddenly aware that his objective wasn't Colette Esterhazy any longer. She had been pretty free with her favours, even allowing for the fact that she was under the influence of Lourdais. Leygues. Courtrand. The man at the University. It could have been me, he thought, if I'd met her earlier. But it didn't matter now whether she was as honest as he hoped or whether she'd been leading him up the garden path or not. Nosjean wanted to forge on, not to conjecture. He had to telephone Paris.

Leygues was in his office when Nosjean and Regnard arrived at the Musée des Arts Modernes. It was late in the evening and Regnard had hurtled down at a dangerous speed on the wintry roads from Paris. It was already late but Nosjean knew he would find Leygues at the museum because he had an apartment off the main hall.

With the heat on, the museum was like an oven after the cold. It was Distaing who let them in. The *gardiens* all did a night watch and it was Distaing's turn. He looked faintly sheepish.

'I went to see her in prison,' he admitted.

'So I gathered,' Nosjean said. 'I saw your portrait.'

Leygues was in his office, which was full of pictures. They filled every bit of space and leaned five or six deep against the wall. Leygues was on the telephone and he waved to Nosjean to sit down.

Nosjean waited patiently until the call ended and Leygues straightened up. He introduced Regnard. 'This is Sergeant Regnard from Paris,' he said. 'He's investigating the death of a man called Patrick Lourdais.'

Leygues' smooth pink face showed a disdainful lack of interest. 'I'm afraid I don't know the gentleman,' he said.

'He's an artist. He was shot two days ago in his studio.'

'I see. And what has this to do with me?'

'I've just come from seeing Colette Esterhazy.'

A flicker of expression ran across Leygues' features. Pain? Nosjean wondered. Anger? Bewilderment? It was hard to say.

'She's been telling me about Lourdais. I suppose you've read the papers?'

Leygues sat at his desk, frowning. 'I don't know him,' he repeated.

'I think you know *of* him.'

'He's an unknown, surely? He's not in any catalogue I've read.'

'Colette Esterhazy lived with him.'

Again the fleeting expression of pain crossed Leygues' face.

'He was the man who put her up to stealing the Rousseau and the Paot. Surely you guessed that?'

'Why should I? I didn't know the man.'

'No? Have you got the pictures back?'

'How could I have?'

'Because you shot him, didn't you?' said Nosjean very gently, and he waited patiently for the shock to take effect.

Leygues sat very still for what seemed a very long while. 'Why do you say that?' he asked eventually, his voice composed as if he was asking the most casual of questions.

'She was your mistress, wasn't she? She slept with you.' Nosjean began to rap out statements, putting the pressure on now, hoping that Leygues would break. 'He persuaded her to. So you'd agree to take the pictures out of the frames for her. They'd be light and easy to carry. You knew of him. You were trying to persuade her to leave him for you.' Nosjean paused for breath, wondering if he was having the required effect. 'Did you hope to put her in your debt long enough for her to change her mind? When the pictures disappeared, you knew where they'd gone, who had them. And, unlike me, you knew his name, so you managed to find out where he was.'

'I have to ask,' Regnard said, moving forward, doing his bit to put on the pressure, 'do you possess a pistol? Belgian .38?'

Leygues sat stock still for a moment. 'I have no pistol,' he said slowly. 'I did have a .38 Belgian pistol. I was allowed a licence in view of the treasures we have here.'

'Where is it now?'

Leygues remained silent for a while then he drew a deep breath. 'I threw it in the Seine from the Pont St Louis.'

'And the pictures?' Nosjean asked quietly. They were there now, he knew they were there. A tingle of excitement pulsed through him. This was why he was a policeman – he knew that. He was a policeman regardless of climaxes like this.

Leygues rose and, taking a key from his waistcoat pocket, went to a cupboard at the back of the room. Unlocking it, he reached inside.

The pictures glowed as Leygues carefully brought them out and propped them against the wall so that the light from a standard lamp fell on them. It was the first time that Nosjean had seen the originals and he caught his breath. They were so clearly alive and so wholly fresh.

'They're back where they belong,' Leygues said unemotionally.

'What did you intend to do with them?' Nosjean asked. 'You could never have put them on exhibition.' The excitement was still there but subsiding like a satisfying orgasm.

Leygues sat still again, not moving, not a muscle flickering. 'No,' he said eventually. 'No. Probably not. It was all so pointless, really. I couldn't have hidden them for ever.'

Regnard stepped towards him briskly. 'I'm going to charge you with the murder of Patrick Lourdais, sir,' he said. 'I'm afraid you'll have to come with me to Paris.'

'Do I have to?' Leygues said. 'I don't really like Paris. That's why I moved down here.' He gave a gentle, reflective smile.

'The case belongs to Paris,' Nosjean explained. 'There's no choice.'

'Of course. I understand.' Leygues sighed and looked at Nosjean. 'Colette's so beautiful, isn't she, Sergeant? She has a rare light to her – as if she *comes* from a painting. Do you see what I mean? Or do you think I'm a romantic fool?'

'You're not a fool.' Nosjean was adamant. 'Not a fool at all.'

Nosjean handed his report on Colette Esterhazy to Pel, still not certain how entirely truthful she had been. Of course he had got his man. But he wasn't sure about his woman. 'I've spoken to the Palais de Justice,' he said. 'They think she'll get away with nothing more than probation.'

'Is that what you think she deserves, *mon brave*?' Pel asked.

Nosjean wasn't sure. He had gone home thankfully to Mijo, drained of emotion. 'I think that just about fits the bill.'

Pel raised his eyebrows at his colleague's confidence. He sounded far too certain. But Pel didn't want to probe. Nosjean was an intuitive policeman and therefore invaluable. But with intuition went emotion and Pel accepted that.

True to form, Nosjean left Pel's office still doubtful. Was Colette Esterhazy clever or was she just naïve? He supposed he'd never find out now and there was something horribly unsatisfactory about that. The sense of anticlimax in him began to increase.

Pel watched him leave. He knew what Nosjean was going through. Perhaps because he had three sisters, he was always a pushover where the delicate emotions of a woman were concerned. It was the one thing that would prevent him ever becoming a top cop, for he had far more brains and perception than his team mate, De Troq. But

De Troq's ambitions were different. He would retire quite happily on the laurels he'd collected, indifferent to what rank he had. After all, he had a title so it didn't matter much. Nosjean was probably cleverer even than Darcy. But Darcy was always the better cop because he had a tougher mind and didn't get involved.

Pel sighed and moved the files on his desk. Though, morally, she probably wasn't as perfect as she was physically – or as perfect as Nosjean felt she was – Colette Esterhazy had undoubtedly been led astray by a conniving and greedy man. Without doubt the magistrates would be lenient because it was a first offence. But what a first offence. Probably they would be lenient to Leygues, too – even to Morell's Guy Loisel and René Carrera because they were young and their motives had not been pure greed.

Nosjean and Morell, Pel decided, had done well, much better than he was doing. Their cases had much to do with the emotions, while he was dealing with a beautifully conceived plan that also seemed to be flawless in its execution. He and Darcy were still wallowing in doubtful clues and dead-end enquiries and he had a grim feeling that every day he somehow went a step back.

They had followed every lead they had, but had produced nothing from either the equipment or the map the bank robbers had used. There had been no fingerprints anywhere, and even the print of a shoe on the sheet of bank notepaper hadn't led them anywhere. Footprints didn't, unless you had the shoe and knew the owner. They were like fingerprints. They were fine for identifying people but, unless the quarry was in the records, they led you nowhere. And, with Meluc dead, the one man who knew the robbers was gone.

It led him to do a lot of thinking.

Even Annie Saxe had got her man, he thought. The

Guillets, both on crutches, both, as good twins will, with one foot in plaster, had already appeared before the magistrates. They would *not* end up bound over because they had been in trouble before.

The one thing that was common to them all, it seemed, was devotion. Morell's boys had stolen because their grandmother was housebound and they had thought a video would keep her entertained. Colette Esterhazy had stolen the pictures for the love of a man who had turned out to be a rogue and who had deserted her as soon as he'd got them. François Guillet had tried to free his brother for no other reason than that they were twins. Quite a series of cases, Pel thought cynically. Love conquers all. They were all devoted to someone.

He sat up sharply. Devoted? That was the common denominator. They were all *devoted* to someone. It sounded in his mind like the bleep of a cash register. Devoted.

'This Dufrenic type,' he asked Darcy. 'The one who worked for the sewerage department. Was he bumped off? Or did he die a natural death?'

'Natural death,' Darcy said. 'I checked. Cancer. Aged fifty-five. Mid-November. Apparently he knew he was going to die – knew he only had a few weeks. He had a lot of pain, but the only person who knew was his wife. She's a bit of a cripple and he'd done everything for her for years.'

'Héloise and Abélard types. Devoted. Till death us do part. What did he do for the sewerage people?'

'He worked underground for a time. Later he got a job in the office. He would have had access to the maps but the gang would have needed the advice of a policeman to have helped with the diagram of the traffic deviation.'

'What else do we know about Dufrenic?'

'He was decently educated, but he worked in a circus for a while, as some kind of clown. He did an act called The Man in a Bottle. Wriggled his way into a large glass jar or something. He stuck at that until he was around forty then he seems to have gone a bit astray. Perhaps he was growing stiff and wriggling into a jar was too much like hard work. Then he was hauled in for the bank job in Reims and he did four years.'

'Then what?'

'There's a bit of a blank when he came out but five years later he turns up working for the sewerage department. Then an injury he'd suffered in the circus began to trouble him and they put him in the office. He wasn't any kind of expert, Benoist says. He just did minor clerical stuff. Apparently they didn't want to pension him off so he did the running about. Fetching and carrying. Handling the files. Bringing the plans and documents that were wanted up from the basement and putting them away again. They say he insisted on carrying on doing this even when he was ill. They knew his record but they felt he was safe. Nobody thought sewers could be criminal.'

'Do they have copying machines?'

'Who doesn't these days? They use them for copying plans.'

Pel sniffed. He could say a lot with a sniff. This one expressed satisfaction. 'Devotion,' he muttered.

That afternoon, Pel got Annie Saxe to drive him to the cemetery. The snow was thick on the ground and nobody seemed to have been there before them because the only tracks were those of birds and cats. The *gardien* looked in his book for the position of the grave they were seeking.

'Plot 7,' he said. 'Row 12. Number 34. It's right over by

the wall. It's a bit of a lost part of the cemetery there. The widow visits it quite a lot, though.'

They tramped through the snow and stopped before a tomb that looked like a huge over-decorated telephone booth, with cast-iron gates designed to look like crude wrought-iron. In a glass-fronted frame on the front was a photograph which showed a thin-faced man with a sardonic expression, his hair flattened down from a centre parting. Below, the legend ran *Sacred to the memory of Josip, beloved husband of Gabrielle*. There was a bunch of wax flowers under a glass dome and fresh ones sprinkled with snow in a porcelain jar.

They could also make out the interior beyond the iron gates. It contained a slab of marble let into the ground, and on one side there was a coffin with a small vase on top containing fresh flowers.

'Don't they bury them here?' Pel asked. 'And fresh flowers? Inside? How did they get there?'

The *gardien* gave them the answer. 'She puts them there,' he said.

'Who does?'

'The widow.'

'Why isn't the coffin in the vault?'

'It is.'

'We saw it. It's against the law to leave a coffin like that.'

'That's empty.'

'Empty?'

'It's for her when her time comes. She says it's there so he'll know he's not forgotten.'

'She put flowers on it. Aren't the gates kept locked?'

'She has a key and she's quite entitled to unlock them. She likes to have them open. She likes to talk to him.'

'She talks to him?' Pel was a little surprised.

'I've heard her. Sometimes she even brings a folding chair and sits there.'

'What does she talk about?'

'Oh, things. Old times. Circuses mostly, it seems. They were both in a circus. She calls him Jo-Jo. Sometimes I half expect him to answer.'

'How long has she been doing this?'

'A few weeks now. Perhaps she's going . . .' The *gardien* touched his temple. 'You know how people go when they're lonely. It's not too bad at first but then, after a while it starts to bite, I find. We get some funny types. She's quite harmless and nobody goes down there these days.'

'Why was he buried there, then?'

'His wife asked for it. She said he liked space and wasn't used to having a lot of people round him. Perhaps she opens the gates so he can hear her better.'

This was a new one to Pel.

'What's she like?'

The *gardien* gestured. 'Fifty-ish,' he said. 'Big woman. Lame legs. Limps badly.'

Pel turned to Annie. 'I wonder where the money came from to build a sepulchre like this?'

Annie looked puzzled and she stamped her cold feet in the snow. 'What are we looking for?' she asked.

'A criminal,' Pel said. 'And I think we've found him.'

'Where?'

'Right in front of you. You're looking at the man who master-minded that Crédit Rural job. He must have planned it all and then died before it could be pulled off.'

Annie stared at him. 'You're pulling my leg, sir.'

'No, I'm not. And then the rest of the gang carried out the robbery after his death and paid his share to the wife. He must have had a lot of guts and anyway, maybe he wanted to leave his wife a small fortune. That's devotion, isn't it? He looks after her for years and then he gets the chance to secure her future – knew he was dying so he took one big, wonderful opportunity. Why have I been so damned blind? He knew exactly where the sewers ran. I bet in his time he examined the cellars of every bank in the city. I can also bet he died smiling.'

'Isn't this all speculation?' Annie asked.

'Yes, but I know I'm right. The evidence was all there – sitting with Darcy. I just didn't ask him, and he didn't connect it with anything.'

'Well,' Annie said, 'we can't arrest Dufrenic. That's for sure. So what now?'

'We ought to be able to get leads on the gang – and the ex-cop, if there is one.'

'The wife?'

'She'll tell us. It'll come out if we work hard enough on her. I reckon once Dufrenic got hooked into the underworld in Reims, he never left it. Just think of it. Suggestions from the Sepulchre. Guidance from the Grave.' It sounded like a cheap thriller.

Annie looked at Pel shrewdly. 'You still can't prove anything. So if Madame doesn't co-operate . . .'

'She will,' said Pel reflectively. 'She'll damn well have to.'

Madame Dufrenic lived in the basement of a modest house with shutters by a small park on the edge of town. She was badly crippled and overweight and lived in dusty squalor. Pel could see that the basement had once been a place of comfort, a bolt-hole from a hostile world, for the walls were hung with good Impressionist and Expressionist paintings as well as innumerable little models of various sculptural works of art. Where there weren't paintings, there were circus photographs – clowns, acrobats, trapeze artists, contortionists.

She looked so terrified that Pel would have been inclined to put her out of her misery at once, but he had to be sure and this meant building the situation up to such a height that she would eventually fall from their mutually constructed cliff.

'Madame Dufrenic?'

'Yes.' She had walked with a stick when she had let him in and there had been a brief silence while he surveyed the apartment and she painstakingly closed the front door.

'Your husband was a contortionist, I believe.'

'Many years ago.' Her voice was so soft that he could hardly hear her and suddenly a loathing for what he was about to do – for what he had done so many times before – came over him. Why did he go on doing this job? And if he was going to, why couldn't he delegate, get someone else to do it? Someone more sympathetic like Annie Saxe. But he knew why, knew that he always carried out his own dirty work.

'I didn't quite hear what you said.'

'He was a contortionist, many years ago.'

'In a circus?'

'Yes.'

'And yourself? Is that where you met?'

'I worked with the horses. But I had a fall.'

'Is that what crippled you?' he asked slowly.

'Yes.'

'And he cared for you all those years?'

'He did. Monsieur, you say you are a policeman. Can you tell me why you wish to see me?'

'It is about your husband, as I said on your doorstep.'

'But to be specific – *what* about him?' Her voice shook.

'Please, madame. Let me do it my way.'

'What are you building up to?'

'Madame, I do *need* to do it my way.' He smiled at her, sure in the knowledge that he had solved the case. He would be gentle with her, he promised himself, providing she didn't go stubborn on him, and if she did, it would be his own fault.

'Very well.'

'I gather he worked in the sewers.'

'Yes.'

'No doubt his former profession as a contortionist assisted him in his work.'

'No doubt.'

'But, like you, he sustained an injury.'

'He hurt his back.'

'And that forced him to take an office job – with the sewerage company.'

'Yes.'

'He knew he was going to die. How was that?'

'The doctor told him.'

'The back injury?'

'He had cancer in his bones. He didn't have long.'

'I see. Madame . . .' Pel paused but more for effect than anything else. Again, a wave of self-loathing consumed him. 'Was he worried about leaving you badly provided for?'

'He had savings,' she said woodenly.

'Enough to keep you in comfort?'

'Not comfort.'

'To provide for your needs?'

She paused. 'I can live simply. Look around you.'

'Is your condition deteriorating, madame?'

'It's stable.'

'Would you mind if I had you medically examined?'

'You mean you have the right?' she asked.

'I have the right.'

'There's no need for your examination,' she said patiently. 'I *am* deteriorating.'

'You need nursing help?'

'If I wish to stay in my own home.'

'And do you?'

She looked around her with a hopeless air and Pel knew that it would not be long before she gave in. 'We've been here twenty-five years, Josip and I. If I went into a nursing home, or hospital, I think it would kill me. I feel him here still.' She paused. 'He's with me.'

'You go to the sepulchre a good deal?'

'Yes.'

'Your own coffin's there?'

'It is.'

'And you talk to Josip?'

'Who told you that?'

'The *gardien*.'

'You *have* been making enquiries.' She smiled for the first time and Pel knew that it was a smile of relief. Josip had provided for her so well that she was clearly terrified, probably all day and all night. They wouldn't do much to her, Pel thought. But where would she end up? Probably just where she dreaded – and what could he do about that? Nothing.

'Yes, I talk to him. It brings me comfort.'

'That sepulchre. It must have cost a lot. It's very grand.'

'Josip had savings.'

'As much as that?'

'That's what he wanted,' she said placidly.

'Couldn't the money have been better spent – on nursing care for you, for instance?'

'He had savings.' She was dogged now.

'*More* savings? Do you have a nurse?'

'The district nurse comes in.'

'No one else?'

'No one.' Perhaps she was afraid to touch the money. Or maybe she was only going to do so when time had passed.

'But surely you need more than ... cursory treatment?'

She shook her head. 'I can get by.'

'For how long?'

She didn't reply and Pel cast an obvious eye around the room. Madame Dufrenic followed his gaze. 'I'm not up to doing much cleaning.'

'You can't afford it?'

She raised her eyebrows. 'Monsieur Pel, you must tell me why you are here. I think you have taken time enough leading up, don't you?'

He bowed. 'Yes, madame. I have reason to believe your husband was involved in a very substantial bank robbery. In fact, I believe he master-minded it.'

'That is a very alarming proposition.'

'Nevertheless I have evidence to support it.'

She looked at him shrewdly but said nothing.

'Madame, I believe it would be a relief for you to unburden yourself. I'm sure you'll not be prosecuted, and I'm equally sure that you have left your own share – your husband's share – quite untouched. Except, of course, for the sepulchre.'

'Just supposing you were right, monsieur, is it likely that the sepulchre would be torn down?'

'I think it's a little too late for that.'

'Are you certain?' She looked at him almost threateningly.

'I would use all my influence and I'm sure I could be certain. Besides, it's a very fine job and I'm sure the church authorities would back me up.'

Madame Dufrenic visibly relaxed. 'What do you want to know?'

'Did he do it?'

'Yes, but to provide for me. Do you believe that?'

'He *did* know he was going to die?'

'Certainly.'

'Then I believe you.' Pel let a short silence develop. Then he said, 'I need some information.'

'What is it?'

'Where is the money?'

'It's under the floorboards in my bedroom – a traditional hiding place, I'm sure you will say. But Josip died rather more quickly than he had imagined, and final arrangements, like a safe bank account, had not been made. He was not a man very familiar with high finance, as you can imagine.'

'He was more familiar with squeezing into small spaces,' said Pel gently.

'It was his idea. He planned the operation and recruited the men.'

'They carried it out after he died and paid you his share?'

'Of course.'

'And you know who they are?'

'No.'

Pel paused again. It was not going to be easy after all. Heaven knows why he had momentarily expected it to be so. 'Madame, the only way things could go wrong for you – '

'Go wrong?' She was visibly alarmed and looked at him accusingly as if he had reneged on his assurances.

'Would be if you were to withhold evidence.'

'I see.'

'So, do you know who these men are?'

'I told you. No.'

'There is no means of finding out?'

'You can search the place,' she said impatiently, 'but Josip was most meticulous.'

'There are other questions, madame.'

'Yes?'

'Please remember that you *must* answer them truthfully.'

'I will, if I can.'

'There was an ex-cop involved. There had to be.'

She nodded. 'There was.'

'Do you know him?'

'He came here once or twice.'

'Would you recognize him again?' asked Pel a little too eagerly and she smiled at him as if she was indulging a boy.

'Not only would I recognize him, but I know his name.'

'Yes?'

'His name is Bernard Vigo. Do you know him?'

'The name rings a bell.' Pel felt a thrill of delight. What was more, he was certain that she was telling the truth.

'Well, I'm sure you can trace him. But please leave my name out of it, for Josip's sake. Can you guarantee that?'

'Yes, providing you can give me a little more information, madame.'

'I thought you might strike another bargain, monsieur. Is this the nature of your stock in trade?' She looked at him contemptuously and Pel squirmed.

'Yes, I'm afraid it is.'

'Well?'

'It's Meluc. You may not have – '

'I knew him,' she said sharply. 'He was an errand boy.'

'You sound as if you didn't like him.'

'I had no time for him,' she said firmly.

'Why not?'

'He tried to blackmail Josip, just before he died.'

'How?'

'He wanted more of a cut than an errand boy deserves.'

'And?'

'When he was told he couldn't have it, he sulked like a child and then threatened to wreck the whole scheme. So...'

'So Josip had him killed?'

'He wasn't like that.'

'Someone else?'

'Yes.'

'But you don't know who?'

'No, and I mean that.'

'Is this the full extent of your knowledge, madame?'

She nodded. 'I'm holding nothing back.'

'You're certain?'

'Yes.'

'You swear?' Pel wanted to press the point.

'I swear on my husband's sepulchre – and my own. You know how important that is to me, Monsieur Pel.'

'Yes, I know.'

There was a long silence. Then she said. 'He was a good man, my Josip.'

'He was a clever one. A devoted one.'

She smiled happily. 'Shall I show you where the money is?'

Pel strolled away, having summoned assistance and leaving a guard in case the old lady burnt the money or herself or both. He would be able to get some help for her, but wasn't sure if she would take it.

He wanted fresh air and he now walked briskly down the tree-lined avenue. He thought of his own devoted wife and how his home sometimes felt like a trap – a loving trap. Pel decided to lengthen his stroll. Everything could wait.